CASSIE EDWARDS
THE SAVAGE SERIES

Winner of the *Romantic Times* Lifetime Achievement Award for Best Indian Series!

MAKING AMENDS

"Again, I apologize for the wrongs of my father. Had I known then that he had taken you captive, I would have stopped at nothing to save you."

"As you know, I was not his captive for long, so do not despair over it," Misshi said. She turned toward him. She moved to her knees facing him and placed gentle hands on his cheeks. "I was gone from your father's stronghold almost the moment I was taken there. As your father lay on the ground, terribly wounded, no one paid attention to me. It was easy to slip away."

"You were, you still are, a woman of much bravery and heart," Soaring Hawk said. He took her hands from his face, then lowered his mouth to her palms, kissing each.

"I was afraid, oh, so very afraid," Misshi said.

"You never need be afraid again." He reached for her and lifted her so that she was now on his lap. He cradled her close and pressed his nose into the sweet smell of her hair. "I will always be here to protect you."

Cassie Edwards

Savage Moon

LEISURE BOOKS   NEW YORK CITY

A LEISURE BOOK®

February 2002

Published by

Dorchester Publishing Co., Inc.
276 Fifth Avenue
New York, NY 10001

ISBN 0-7394-2321-5

For those of you who read *Savage Devotion,* you remember about Lexi, a Chinese orphan adopted by my heroine in the book. In true life, there is a real Lexi, my two-year-old Chinese granddaughter! I ever so lovingly dedicate *Savage Moon* to my adorable "Chinese princess," Alexis Jade Edwards—Lexi, as well as my son Charles (her father), and daughter-in-law Kathleen (her mother), who went directly to China to adopt Lexi; and also I dedicate this book to my wonderful twenty-one-year-old grandson David.

I wish to add a few more names to this dedication . . . Marilyn McGill, a new dear friend of mine, and another special friend Tammy Russotto, as well as her husband Brian, and daughter Tiffany.

I also dedicate this book to Steve Sandalis, a dear, sweet friend and model who posed for the cover of *Savage Moon,* and his wife Katy, and son Stefan.

I would also like to include John Ennis, the talented artist, who paints fantastic covers for my *Savage* series, in this dedication. Thank you, John.

Why should we flee to foreign lands,
Why should we submit to their demands,
Why should we suffer for their greed,
Because we are not of their breed?
Our ancestors fought to keep this land,
While the Indian makes his last stand.
Much blood was shed,
While the white man's hatred spread.
They look upon us with great disgust.
Because of them we have lost all trust.
I shed tears for my fallen clan.
Like scared rabbits we ran.
They say we are without God,
That our beliefs are odd.
But we know His spirit lives in all.
Why should we worship in a great hall?
The white man's civilization is near;
They will crush what we hold so dear.
We will not bend,
Though we will all suffer in the end.

—Cassandra Olinger

Chapter One

O, World, thou choosest not the better part!
It is not wisdom to be only wise,
And on the inward vision close the eyes;
But it is wisdom to believe the heart.
     —George Santayana
     "O World, thou Choosest Not" (1894)

Wyoming, 1852

The wagon train ambled slowly through the tall, waving grasses, the ten wagons being pulled by five mules each.

One cow, which supplied the travelers with fresh milk, was tied at the back of the very first wagon.

1

The other cows had not survived the journey west.

The cows were not the only victims of the journey. Fresh mounds of dirt along the trail marked the graves of people who had died of illness, sheer exhaustion, and . . . Indian attacks.

Eight-year-old Misshi Bradley sat in her pretty little white cotton dress on the seat of the last wagon. Beside her sat her redheaded, eighteen-year-old brother Dale, who was the only surviving member of her family. Their mother had died some weeks ago while attempting to give birth to her third child. Her mother and the unborn baby lay beneath the ground in an unmarked grave so that Indians would not know where she lay. The travelers had feared they might want her hair to add to their scalp collections.

Tears fell from Misshi's violet eyes as she thought of her beloved father, Virgil Hiram, who had fought so valiantly to protect Misshi and Dale from the savages, only to die when a poison arrow pierced his heart during an Indian attack several days after her mother's death.

Misshi's brother and the other surviving men had chased off the renegades with heavy gunfire so that no one else died that awful day. But ever since then, Misshi had felt that the trail they were following led nowhere but to everyone's eventual death.

2

Trying not to linger on such thoughts, she focused on the loveliness of *this* day. Birds swept down from the heavens singing gentle melodies, and white, fluffy clouds floated like sailboats across the blue sky.

Nearby, buffalo were grazing peacefully, the young calves at their mothers' sides. In the distance a butte was silhouetted against the sky. The intervening country lay in deep, purple shadows, the myriad folds and deep convolutions adding texture to this remarkable landscape.

It was a place of unspoiled beauty, but there was a harshness about this land that frightened Misshi. From time to time she caught sight of large grayback wolves following the buffalo, waiting to pounce upon the young or the wounded. And the sun itself was a constant threat.

Misshi clutched the brim of her sunbonnet now as she tried to protect the tender flesh of her face, but to no avail. Although it was a beautiful day, with a soft breeze blowing the tall grass, the sun was merciless.

Her tender face had been sunburned repeatedly on the long journey from Ohio. She hated the flakes of skin that fell from her face as she scrubbed it each evening before retiring in the back of the wagon with her brother Dale.

Her mother had always said that being a redhead

made her more vulnerable to the sun than other women. Her skin was much fairer than theirs.

Misshi had been aggravated by her freckles ever since the first time she had looked into a mirror. She had detested the sight of them even though she was only three and did not even know the meaning of the word "vain" yet.

Yes, vain, she thought to herself. Her brother had always teased her because she was so particular about her looks.

She glanced over at her brother, pride in her eyes as she saw how straight-backed he sat as he clutched the reins. He had classic features, she thought, features that had attracted many a woman on the wagon train.

But it was his dancing, friendly, grass-green eyes that Misshi loved best. Very rarely did he look at anyone without a smile in those eyes.

It saddened Misshi to think that perhaps neither she nor her brother would make it back to civilization again. But the trail had been too long. There had been too many deaths.

And as they advanced farther and farther into Indian country, their chances of reaching their destination seemed only a dream that had turned into a nightmare.

Wanting to think of pleasant things again, Misshi concentrated on the powerful bond between her and her brother. She smiled as she thought of how she had acquired the name Misshi, when in truth her name was Mitzi. Because her brother could not pronounce her name when she was born—he always called her "Misshi"—her parents had given her that nickname; only a few people even knew that she had another name.

"Misshi, you are in such deep thought," Dale said. "What were you thinking about, little sister, that made you smile so sweetly?"

"You, big brother, *you*," Misshi said.

She laughed softly as she reached over and placed a hand on his knee, the leather fabric of his breeches rough to her fingers. The fabric had gone hard from many washings, and was even cracked in places.

"Maybe I'd best not ask what your thoughts were, but you were smiling, weren't you?" he said, chuckling.

"I was thinking about why I am called Misshi instead of Mitzi," she said, her eyes smiling into his. "I do love the name Misshi, Dale. I just can't see myself as a 'Mitzi,' now can you?"

Instead of answering, Dale looked past her, and then looked over his shoulder as if he was looking for something or someone; Misshi became suddenly afraid. They had come across soldiers yesterday who had stopped the wagon train and warned everyone that a renegade Bannock Indian chief, Chief Bear, was on the loose, killing and maiming and taking white captives.

The soldiers had warned the people of the wagon train to be wary of this crazed Indian. He could be recognized by a drooping eyelid and a livid, jagged scar on the left side of his face, both of which had been caused during his capture a year ago.

Sneaky and clever, Chief Bear had escaped to roam the land again with his evil followers.

Misshi had been disappointed when the soldiers had gone on their way without even offering assistance in getting them safely to their fort. They had said they did not have the time to escort the wagons to safety.

They thought they were on the trail of the renegade chief. They could not chance losing him again.

"Dale, what is it?" Misshi blurted out, as Dale grabbed a rifle from behind him and laid it across his lap.

"I sense danger," he said, then began shouting to everyone to drive the wagons into a wide circle.

"Prepare for an attack!"

Her heart thudding like a thousand drums, Misshi held on to the seat of the wagon for dear life as Dale hastily maneuvered it into the circle.

"Get down!" Dale cried as he leaped from the wagon. "Come on, Misshi. Get down beside me. I'll protect you."

She didn't have the chance to do as he said. Suddenly the Indians appeared from out of no-where. They came in a rush around a bend in the land where they had been lurking in the shadows of trees.

Whooping and hollering, they rode their horses at breakneck speed through the tall grass.

Their volley of arrows slammed into the wagons and some of the mules as they shouted the war cry that was now horribly familiar to Misshi.

She covered her ears with her hands and closed her eyes tightly, afraid to hear or see what was happening, for she knew that in a matter of minutes she and her brother could be two more graves along the trail.

She began praying, then opened her eyes wildly when she heard the thundering of hoofbeats close to her wagon and the shriek of an Indian.

"You bastard!" she heard Dale shout as she felt herself being grabbed off the wagon and thrown across the back of a horse, belly down.

She could hardly believe what was happening to her, yet she knew that some Indian had been bra-zen enough to ride through the heavy gunfire and grab her right before her brother's eyes.

She tried to get free, but a heavy hand was holding her down, while the Indian's other hand held the reins of his steed. He rode away from the wagons in a flurry of gunfire.

When Misshi heard a grunt of pain come from the Indian who held her captive, she knew that one of the bullets had hit home. She had no idea where he'd been hit because she was still immobile on her belly.

"Let me go!" she screamed, kicking and hitting at the Indian's bare legs, for he wore only a brief breechclout and moccasins.

When he shouted threatening-sounding Indian words back at her, she grew quiet, for she did not want to be killed on the spot.

The horse thundered onward alongside the others as they drew farther and farther away from the circle of wagons.

For what seemed an eternity, they rode onward. Then suddenly the horse stopped and her captor threw her to the ground.

As she lay on her back, cowering beneath the glare of the many Indians who were circling around her, she became aware of the man who had taken her captive.

There was no denying his drooping eyelid and livid, jagged scar. It was Chief Bear who had stolen her away from her brother.

She screamed when Chief Bear suddenly slid from his horse and fell down onto the ground, writhing in pain beside her.

When she saw the blood at the base of his skull, she knew where the bullet had entered his flesh.

It was incredible to Misshi how he had had the strength to go on after having been shot in such a way, yet he had. He had stayed in his saddle long enough to get Misshi far away from her people.

She scooted away from the injured chief as his men came and knelt beside him. While they checked his wound, one of the warriors grabbed her by her hair and dragged her over to a horse. He tossed her across it on her belly and tied her securely.

Knowing that she was now at the mercy of these renegades, Misshi silently cried out for her big brother to save her.

Back at the wagon train, Dale was still feeling numb, even speechless, at how quickly his sister had been taken from him.

"It was Chief Bear, the Bannock renegade the soldiers told us about," Dale shouted angrily as the survivors of the attack gathered and stood together.

Dale stared across the blowing grass where he had last seen his sister being taken away on the renegade's horse. "I saw his face," he said aloud. "I saw the scar. I saw the drooping eyelid."

9

He swallowed hard. "It tears at my heart to know that such a man has my sister."

Then his anger peaked. "Damn the soldiers!" he shouted. "They should have seen to our safe arrival at their fort. Now what can we do? There aren't enough of us left to mount a search for my sister."

He turned and stared in another direction. "Surely the fort is out there somewhere," he said. "We must find it and demand that they send out a search party for Misshi."

To himself, he vowed that, somehow, he would hunt down Chief Bear and kill the savage himself, then reclaim his sister.

If . . . she . . . was still alive!

Chapter Two

There is no feeling in a human
heart which exists in that heart
alone—which is not, in some
form or degree, in every heart.
—George Macdonald
"Unspoken Sermons" (1885)

High in the mountains at a Bannock Indian
stronghold, there was an air of mixed sadness and
excitement as Soaring Hawk sat with his mother,
White Snow Feather. Soaring Hawk's father, Chief
Bear, was away doing what he did best, terrorizing
innocent travelers who were crossing land that he
felt belonged to the red man.

11

"*Peta*, my child, it is time today, while your father is gone, to leave with those braves that you have chosen to form your own band of Bannocks," White Snow Feather said as she sat beside the fire in their lodge.

"But, Mother, when I leave, I leave *you* behind," Soaring Hawk said, his voice full of concern for the mother he adored. "You know that when Father finds me gone, he will immediately blame you. I do not wish to think of what he might do to you. Should he lay a hand on you, Mother, I—"

"Son, son, do not worry so much about your mother," White Snow Feather said softly. "I have lived a full, rewarding life. No mother could be as fortunate as I, who have had you for a son. Remember that however your father reacts to your departure, I will be smiling, for I will know that I have done right urging you to go."

Old and tired, her coarse gray hair twisted into a tight bun made of braids at the back of her head, White Snow Feather reached her wrinkled hand over to her handsome young son and patted his bare knee.

"I have done right by you, my son, and you make me proud to know that your beliefs are the same as mine. I know that you will live a righteous life that will make all who know of you, admire you."

Despite her brave words, there was sadness in White Snow Feather's eyes.

Soaring Hawk had been born to her late in life, after she became Chief Bear's fifth wife. She was the only one of his wives to bear him a son, and White Snow Feather knew that her husband would hate her twofold for urging this son to leave their camp.

White Snow Feather, who did not believe in her husband's misguided ideals, knew that she chanced banishment, or even death, for having secretly taught her son to be a good warrior. She had taught him to be a man of decency, of honor, to seek peace.

Not war.

She was proud to know that her son would be nothing like his father, who had formed his own renegade band of Indians. Chief Bear allowed no one from his stronghold, not man, woman or child, to associate with the other Bannock bands, who were kinsmen with the powerful Shoshone tribe.

Chief Bear set down his own rules and he took what he wanted, when he wanted, no matter who died in the process, red-skinned or white. He especially enjoyed stopping the wagon trains of *ta-vois*, white explorers and emigrants, whom he hated with a passion.

Soaring Hawk turned to his mother and sank to

his knees before her. He took her hands in his and gazed intensely into her aged, pale brown eyes. "Mother, come with me," he said, his eyes begging her. "Please come with me."

White Snow Feather fought back the urge to cry, for she knew that the moment was nigh when her son would walk away from her forever.

She forced a soft laugh. "*Huh*, yes, and have this old one in your way as you and your chosen men strengthen your fortress against possible enemies," she said.

She swallowed hard. "Reserve that space in your lodge for a young, vital woman, when you feel the time is right to take a wife," she murmured. "Of course, at your age of fifteen winters, a wife is the last thing on your mind. But believe me, my son, there *will* come a time when the need of a woman warming your blankets will be a force that cannot be denied."

"Mother, it is such a good stronghold that awaits my arrival," Soaring Hawk said, his chest puffing out with pride.

He purposely ignored his mother's reference to women. Although he was considered a brave, not a warrior, because of his youth, he did know the ache that men had for women.

Yet he had the willpower to practice restraint and ignore that hunger until later, when he was a man, and his stronghold was well established.

Then, only then, would he search for that per-fect woman.

"You and the other mothers did well in laying aside a good store of weapons, food, and clothes for our escape," Soaring Hawk said. "It is fortunate that Father waited until I reached my fifteenth birthday before talking about having me join him on his raids against humanity."

"And since you have only recently celebrated that fifteenth birthday, it is imperative that you break away now. You must leave your father's band and your father's leadership," White Snow Feather said as she eased her hands from Soaring Hawk's. "Leave now, son. *Mea*, go. Too much time is being taken today in talk. Slowly, bit by bit, so that nothing has been missed by your father or your friends' fathers, supplies have been taken higher up in the mountains where you have established the stronghold of your Hawk Band."

She reached a hand to Soaring Hawk's face and slowly ran her fingers over his sculpted features, as if to etch the memory of his handsome face into her heart forever.

"Son, your tepee awaits you, as do your friends' own lodges," she murmured. "Soon lodge fires will burn in the firepits. Food that you kill will cook over the flames of the fires. I have taught you not

15

only how to be a strong leader with the right morals, I have also taken the time to teach you the art of cooking, since you and your braves will not have mothers, or daughters, or even cousins to cook for you."

"*Huh*, yes, you have prepared this brave very well for life without a mother," Soaring Hawk said.

He flung himself into her arms and gave her one last desperate hug. "I shall miss you, Mother," he said. "Mother, oh, how I shall miss you."

"It is not good to miss a mother too much," White Snow Feather quietly scolded. "My duty to you, my son, is done. Now your life is yours without a mother's constant fussing over you."

She leaned away from him.

Again she placed a hand on his face. "You will soon realize just how much you enjoy not having a mother around to pester you," she said, laughing softly.

"Mother, I have enjoyed every moment I have had with you, and I will draw from my memories of those times when I find myself lonely for you," Soaring Hawk said.

He gave her another hug, then stood tall in his father's huge skin lodge as his mother pushed herself up before him.

"No more hugs as there should be no more words spoken between us today," White Snow Feather

16

said as she stepped away from him. "I will not go outside to see you ride away, for no matter how much I know this is right for you, I ache inside already from missing you. *Mea*, go, my son. Go now, or I might grab hold of your hands and never let you go again."

Understanding her despair, feeling it himself, Soaring Hawk fought back tears that would make him look childish in the eyes of a mother who saw him now as a man. He smiled at her, then turned and rushed outside the tepee, where his bay mare and the other braves on their steeds awaited him.

Feeling the excitement building inside him to know that he was now his own man, and finally free of his father's bonds, Soaring Hawk swung himself into his saddle. The mothers, the elderly, and the children of the stronghold stood watching as Soaring Hawk and his followers rode off, each knowing very well that they might never see their loved ones again.

They were soon far from the renegade stronghold, climbing higher into the mountain. On his magnificent bay mare, Soaring Hawk was filled with anticipation of what lay ahead for him and his followers.

Their goal was to fight for the good of the Bannock tribe as a whole. It was Soaring Hawk's ambition to try to make up for the harm his renegade father had done.

His only regret was having to leave his beloved mother behind, as well as the mothers of his friends, who would be at the mercy of his father when Chief Bear arrived home and discovered the betrayal.

Soaring Hawk's mother had assured him that whatever she had to endure would be worth it, even death, for she could die with peace in her heart, knowing she had led her son down the right life path. White Snow Feather had told him that she would remain loyal to his father forever, except in this one instance when she had to do what was best for her son.

She had told Soaring Hawk always to remember that bravery was the first virtue among the Bannocks and their kinsmen the Shoshone, and that it took much bravery for Soaring Hawk to go against his father, to become a man in his own right.

As Soaring Hawk and his friends rode higher and higher into the mountains, their stronghold only a short distance away now, Chief Bear and his warriors were just arriving home.

When White Snow Feather heard the noise of horses galloping into the stronghold, her insides went cold, for she knew that the coming confrontation with her husband might be the worst of her life.

He might grow so angry that he would thrust a knife deep into her heart.

Ever since she had heard Soaring Hawk ride from the stronghold, she had sat beside her lodge fire, praying. She had prayed for the safety of her son. She had prayed for the understanding of her husband.

Soon she would know whether the latter prayer would be answered. She held her chin high and left the lodge to face her husband.

When she got outside she saw a travois being dragged behind a horse. With dawning horror, she recognized the horse as her husband's. When she saw the lifeless body on the travois, the color drained from her face, for she knew that the one lying there was her *kumaxp*, her husband.

She glanced up at the warrior who rode beside her husband's horse, holding the reins.

"He is not dead," the warrior said.

Sighing with relief, for she did love the man no matter the havoc he wreaked everywhere he went, she fell to her knees beside the travois when the horse came to a halt.

She let out a cry when she saw that Bear was unconscious and there was dried blood on his buckskin shirt.

A warrior fell to his knees beside White Snow Feather. He took her by the hand and talked softly to her. "While taking a young white girl captive, Chief Bear was shot at the base of his skull," he explained as the village people crowded around their fallen chief. "I am not sure if he will live or die."

Those words sounded to White Snow Feather as though they had been spoken from some deep, dark tunnel. She was in a state of shock, unable even to comprehend what the warrior had said about the white captive.

With everyone focusing on Chief Bear, tending his wound with cobwebs and the fine inner bark of trees to stop the bleeding that had just begun anew, Misshi found herself alone on the horse.

A few miles back, the warrior had untied the ropes that had held her onto the steed. They had stopped long enough to drink from a stream, and to wash the blood from their chief's wound. Their full attention on their chief, they had not tied Misshi again.

Now she saw a sudden opportunity for escape. Although she did not know this land at all, especially the dangerous slopes of this mountain, this might be her only chance to escape. Slowly she slid from the horse to the ground.

Her eyes went guardedly from person to person,

to see if anyone was looking at her. When she saw that all eyes were still on their fallen chief, she broke into a mad run and soon found herself amid dense trees, surrounded by the sweet smell of cedar.

"Please, God, let me get safely away from them," she whispered, panting hard as she ran faster and faster down the mountainside.

She was afraid to look over her shoulder.

She was afraid that she would see a renegade in pursuit of her.

Chapter Three

The ruling passion, be it what it will,
The ruling passion conquers reason still.
— Alexander Pope
"Moral Essays" (1731–1735)

Ten years later

It was *Pe-tai-chin-cha-ton*, the buffalo calf moon. As
all of his warriors moved into the council house
for a special gathering with their chief, Soaring
Hawk stood on a nearby bluff.

His waist-length black hair fluttered in the wind
behind him as Soaring Hawk looked out across the
land below. He was turning over many things in

23

his mind, for only yesterday the warrior he had assigned to scout the surrounding area had returned with news that was not good.

The scout was Lone Wolf, Soaring Hawk's favored warrior and devoted friend. As Lone Wolf had mingled with others at a trading post, where both white-skins and red-skinned people gathered to trade and talk, he had heard mention of Soaring Hawk's mother. It was said she was gravely ill.

Soaring Hawk did not put much credence in things said among those who spent their idle time in gossip. Yet how could he ignore the possibility that his mother might be ill?

Lone Wolf had said the man who brought the news was an Indian who seemed somehow familiar. He seemed to know the face from his past, and guessed that the man might be one of Chief Bear's renegades.

Soaring Hawk had to wonder if this warrior might have followed Lone Wolf to the trading post and purposely planted the seed inside his heart about a woman Soaring Hawk loved almost as much as life itself, so that he might take the news back to Soaring Hawk?

Was it a trap of sorts, to draw Soaring Hawk from the safety of his stronghold, to seek truth in the gossip?

Ten long years had passed since he had said that

sad farewell to his mother. Even then he had known that probably they would never see one another again.

But now?

If she *was* ill?

Should he . . . ?

He sighed heavily and thought back over the years since his flight from his father's stronghold. Soaring Hawk had established his band in a naturally formed fortified position in the mountains. From this stronghold, he and his assigned sentries could protect those they loved from the approach of all enemies.

Soaring Hawk was proud of his Hawk Band, and of this land that had been so good to them. In these haunts, where his warriors and their families lived and roamed without interference from the outside world, were mountain lions, wolf, lynx, wildcat, black- and white-tailed deer, antelope, elk, and moose.

The foothills of his stronghold were a hunter's paradise.

Farther up in the lofty mountains, the horned sheep made their home, while in the fastness of the peaks were found the silver-tip grizzly bear, a big prize for an ambitious man.

The warm valleys with their wealth of brilliant

flowers offered wild fruits and streams filled with fish.

And his Hawk Band had many horses, both wild ones that they had captured and those they had stolen from both whites and redskins. He was proud of the massive herd, especially those that he and his warriors had stolen, for it was valorous to steal horses.

He turned and gazed at the large council house, made of wood and buckskin. In the center of the round roof, smoke spiraled lazily from within, where the council fire burned in the firepit of the large, conical-shaped room.

Before going into the lodge himself, Soaring Hawk smiled and nodded at one warrior and then another as they paused to quietly address their chief.

Most of his warriors' lives had been enriched since that day when they had galloped away from his father's stronghold. Many had left their encampment long enough to seek and find wives. They now could boast of many new additions to their band, both wives and children.

But Soaring Hawk had not chosen a wife yet. He was an intense leader, devoted only to his people.

To all who knew him, Chief Soaring Hawk was the perfect Bannock prince.

Huh, he was devoted to his small group of Bannocks, but he had decided to leave his stronghold more often now, to wander and watch for that perfect woman who could brighten his lodge with her smile.

He hungered for a woman for more reasons than that. He had sensual yearnings that had been neglected for too long.

And with a woman at his side, giving him the nourishment of her love, could he not be twice the leader he was said to be today?

Soaring Hawk's thoughts returned to that time long years ago when he had turned his back on his father to become a chief himself, one stronger than Chief Bear and more respected.

He had received word shortly after his flight that his father had been injured, and that his injury had weakened him significantly. Chief Bear had not harmed Soaring Hawk's mother, nor the other mothers who had assisted the young braves.

Soaring Hawk had learned that even after his father was well enough to ride and raid again, he had not even tried to find Soaring Hawk. To Chief Bear, his son was dead for having betrayed him.

Soaring Hawk had heard that no one even dared to speak Soaring Hawk's name in the old chief's presence, or the speaker would be put to death.

It saddened Soaring Hawk to know that he had

caused such hatred in his father. It seemed his anger had sent Chief Bear into a frenzy of murderous raids, raids that Soaring Hawk could no longer ignore. He knew that meeting with his father would be useless. Chief Bear never listened to anyone, least of all a son he hated.

Soaring Hawk had no choice but to challenge his father. Chief Bear's marauding ways were going to get all the Indians in the area involved in a war with the cavalry.

The council that was to be held today was for the purpose of planning how Chief Bear could be stopped.

Soaring Hawk regretted that his father might die in the process, yet he feared that nothing less than death could stop his father's evil ways.

"Soaring Hawk, all are assembled," Lone Wolf said as he stepped up beside his chief. "Everyone awaits your arrival in the council house."

Soaring Hawk inhaled a deep breath, turned and smiled at Lone Wolf, then walked with him to the council house.

Side by side they entered, then seated themselves at the head of the half circle of warriors who sat on spread blankets around the lodge fire.

Some wore scant breechclouts, others wore full buckskin attire, and some wore fringed breeches with a blanket draped loosely around their bare shoulders.

"My warriors, this council was called to discuss my father and to make plans to stop his marauding ways, but instead, I wish to discuss my mother," Soaring Hawk said. "My heart is heavy, for Lone Wolf overheard bad news at the trading post. It is said that she is quite ill. I do not know now what to do. Should I find a way to go to her, to give her a son's love and comfort during her illness? Or should I let our last good-bye stand, since we both knew then that it was unlikely we would meet again in this life? I am so tempted . . ."

"I, too, have given this much thought," Lone Wolf said, drawing all eyes to him. "My chief, my friend, my brother, when we left our mothers behind to come and make a place where we could have our own families and a life that would make us proud, we all said that same sad good-bye. Each of us has wondered, from time to time, what might have happened to our mothers. Yet we know that seeking the truth might bring harm to our wives, who are now mothers in their own right. Still, I understand that this new information urges you to your mother's side."

"I cannot put everyone in danger only because the boy in me wants to go to my mother," Soaring Hawk replied. "The warrior in me knows it is best that I ignore the gossip about White Snow Feather, even if my presence might give her a measure of joy before she dies."

"I can see how torn you are," Lone Wolf said, putting a gentle hand on Soaring Hawk's shoulder. "I have a suggestion that may help lift some of your burden."

"And that is?" Soaring Hawk said thickly.

"Go and meet with Chief Washakie, the powerful Shoshone chief," Lone Wolf said. "He is your close friend and ally. You can tell Chief Washakie of this dilemma. His voice alone is like a balm to one's soul. Washakie will advise you wisely as well as comfort you."

"*Huh*, you are right, and there is still daylight enough for me to go to him today," Soaring Hawk said. He looked from warrior to warrior. "I apologize for having brought you into the council house for naught. I had thought we would smoke, talk, and feast until final plans were made to stop the renegades. But as it is, my heart is too heavy."

"We have waited this long to complete our plans. It will not hurt to wait awhile longer," another warrior said, bringing grunts and nods of agreement from the others. "Go to Washakie. Let him help lift the burden of despair from your heart. Your warriors will await your return."

"Thank you all," Soaring Hawk said. "I will go

to Washakie. His words are the wisest of them all. His love is sincere. I will leave his lodge a better, calmer man."

He turned to Lone Wolf and embraced him. "Thank you, my devoted friend, for always knowing what is best for me."

"Go and find the peace you seek. Whatever you decide to do about your mother, we will follow," Lone Wolf said, rising as Soaring Hawk got to his feet.

They left the council house together, trailed by the other warriors.

Soaring Hawk turned to his men, who now all stood outside the council house facing him. "I shall not be long," he said. "My place is here with you."

He gave them all one last look, then hurried to the horse corral behind his tepee, where his best horses were kept.

He saddled his favorite steed, a strawberry roan. His bay mare had been replaced by this nobler, more muscular and dependable steed five winters ago, yet his bay mare, a friend forever, still mingled among his other horses.

Soaring Hawk swung around and gazed at his people, who stood in the center of the village watching him. He did not like what he saw in their eyes. It was a trace of fear, which he had not seen since their establishment in this stronghold.

31

He felt guilty for bringing this fear, as slight as it was, into their lives. He realized that he could not risk a visit to his mother, yet he still needed the comforting words that Chief Washakie always gave him when he was troubled about one thing or another.

He wheeled his horse around and rode off, soon finding himself descending a steep path that led down one side of the mountain.

As he rode, his horse's hooves slipped and slid, scattering rocks down the steep mountainside.

The sound of the stones reminded him of a tradition his people practiced when someone was ill. He dismounted and knelt on the ground. Picking up several stones, he slid them into one of the two travel bags that always hung across the back of his horse behind his saddle. After getting several stones, he resumed his travel toward Washakie's village.

He smiled when he thought of how Washakie's stronghold had been established out in the open for everyone to see. *Ka*, no, it was not a stronghold. Washakie had no reason to make a home in hiding, because no one saw him as an enemy. He was a man of peace.

Soaring Hawk was a man of peace, as well, but it was different for him. He had been raised by a thieving renegade, and there were some who might see him in the same light only because he was his father's son. Until all knew his peaceful intentions, he had to keep his people safely hidden on the mountain.

Soaring Hawk traveled awhile longer, then began stopping here and there along the trail to deposit stones at different intervals. By doing this, he was creating "medicine piles," the idea being that just as he left rocks behind on his journey, the sickness that was troubling his mother would also be left behind.

After the last rock was in place, Soaring Hawk traveled onward with a lighter heart, yet he still missed his mother today as never before since their last good-byes.

Chapter Four

O spirit of love! how quick and fresh art thou,
That, notwithstanding thy capacity
Recciveth as the sea, naught enters there,
Of what validity and pitch soe'er
But falls into abatement and low price,
Even in a minute; so full of shapes is fancy,
That it alone is high fantastical.
                              —Shakespeare
                              "Twelfth Night," Act I

Dressed in a lovely fringed buckskin dress that was
ornamented with elks' teeth, and wearing ankle-
high moccasins that she had made for herself, Mis-

shi Bradley, now eighteen, felt an excitement today that she could hardly quell.

It was her last day in the menstrual lodge of the Shoshone Indians, with whom she had lived these past ten years. While waiting in the tiny, one-room lodge for her monthly flow to cease, she had spent her time sewing a new doeskin dress and thinking deep thoughts. At night she dreamed wondrous dreams.

Her eyes danced excitedly as she prepared herself to leave the lodge, stuffing her belongings in a parfleche bag. She was still entranced by the dreams that she had experienced while she had been cooped up all alone in the menstrual hut.

She had dreamed of the same warrior with the same handsome face many nights, and she knew the source of her dream. Chief Soaring Hawk.

It had been he who had kept her company in her dreams while she had been alone.

Surely the dreams had meant something.

Surely his returning image meant they were destined for one another, for he was not yet wed, and nor was she.

Because Soaring Hawk's father was the renegade chief who had abducted her, she had been purposely kept from the young man's sight whenever he visited the Shoshone village where Misshi had lived since her escape.

No, Chief Soaring Hawk had never seen Misshi when he visited his friend Washakie, but today she hoped to encourage her chief to change his mind about this. For if she never came face to face with Soaring Hawk, how could her dreams come true?

After sliding a hairbrush made of porcupine quills and pine cones into her bag, Misshi grabbed up the sack and looped the handle over her left arm, but she did not leave right away.

She found herself recalling the way she had first entered this village. After successfully escaping from Chief Bear, Misshi had wandered alone for several days. Hungry and desperately afraid, she had been rescued on the seventh day by Chief Washakie.

Dehydrated, her skin ripped by briars and cactus, her clothes filthy and in tatters, she had been taken by Washakie to his Shoshone village, and then to the lodge of his widowed cousin, whose children were grown and gone.

After studying Misshi's sad, lonely, and dirty face, Pretty Heart had taken pity on Misshi. From that day forth, she had cared for Misshi as though she were her very own child.

She had showered the girl with love until two winters ago when Pretty Heart passed on to the other side, to join her ancestors in the sky.

Shoshone custom dictated that no one live in a

lodge where someone had died, so Misshi had vacated Pretty Heart's lodge and moved into her own brand new tepee, which the warriors of the village had erected for her.

When she'd first arrived in the village, Washakie had sent warriors to look for the wagon train, but there had been no signs of it, or those traveling on it. It was as if all had disappeared into thin air.

She had concluded that she would never see her brother again. She truly believed that now, for ten years had passed without a trace of her brother.

But Misshi would always feel deep gratitude to Chief Washakie, who had become a father figure to her through the years. And it seemed he thought of her as his daughter.

Shoshone custom gave a father the right to barter or dispose of his daughter as he saw fit. Yes, as both her chief and her adopted father now, Washakie had unquestioned authority over her. It was his right to choose the man to whom she would give herself in marriage.

"I want that to be Soaring Hawk," Misshi whispered as she opened the door of the menstrual hut.

As the sun streamed on her face, and the breeze brought with it the smell of the wildflowers that grew in the forest beyond the village, she reveled in the freedom to come and go as she pleased, at least until next month when her monthly flow would send her back inside the menstrual lodge again.

She looked out at the activity in the village. Braves were coming in from the forest, laden with game slung across their shoulders.

Women knelt outside their lodges, some scraping hides, others cooking over their cook fires or sewing in the shade of their tepees.

Children were everywhere, laughing, playing, while their dogs yapped at their heels.

This Shoshone village was a place of two hundred lodges, arranged in such a way that everyone who lived there had access to the stream that wove snake-like along the land beside their village.

The favorite horses of the warriors were in corrals close behind their lodges, while others were in large herds farther away, guarded so that no one could steal them.

Misshi sighed happily. She had adapted well to life with these kind Shoshone. She had even dyed her hair black with the stalks of a root called *we-sha-sha* so that she would look like an Indian. She wore her hair unbraided and parted in the middle.

She was so very fond of her life as an Indian maiden that she was averse to the idea of going back to live in the white world.

But that had not always been so. There had been things that were hard for her to adapt to. The tepee in which she lived was nothing like the cabin where she had once dwelt with her family. And the first time a slain beaver had been served for supper, Misshi had felt nauseous. And parts of buffalo were eaten raw. The gristle of the snout made her ill even now as she thought of it.

No. She had never gotten used to that and even today refused it.

Shuddering, she forced her thoughts to the more pleasant aspects of life as an Indian maiden. She had grown to appreciate most customs of the Shoshone, and she loved Washakie as though he were her very own father.

But she was sorely tired of hiding when other tribesmen or friendly white soldiers visited the village, even though she knew why Washakie asked this of her. He had not wanted Chief Bear to hear where she was, fearing the renegade might retaliate and come to claim her.

Washakie had kept Misshi a secret from everyone but his own people, yet he knew he must allow her to be known soon by other tribes. He had assured her she would not be an old maid. She had just celebrated her eighteenth birthday. Washakie would soon allow her to see men from the other villages.

But there was only one man she wanted to see and that was Soaring Hawk.

With her heart set on talking to Washakie today about Chief Soaring Hawk and her wish to meet him, Misshi broke into a run toward the chief's large tepee.

She was so intent on speaking with him, she did not even hear her name being called by her friends. There was only one thing . . . one person . . . on her mind.

Soaring Hawk!

Chapter Five

For a breeze of morning moves,
And the planet of Love is on high,
Beginning to faint in the light that she loves;
On a bed of daffodil sky.

—Tennyson

Soaring Hawk dismounted at the outskirts of Chief Washakie's village and tethered his strawberry roan in the shade amid tall grass.

As his horse leisurely cropped the grass, Soaring Hawk walked the rest of the way into Washakie's village, his heart heavy with sadness as he continued thinking about his mother.

If someone had purposely spread the word that

43

she was ill to goad Soaring Hawk into doing something that would bring peril to his Hawk Band, he was afraid the scheme might be close to working.

He hoped that under Washakie's guidance he would discover what he should do.

He was so deep in thought, he was not aware of how different his slow gait was from his usual confident, springing steps. With his head hanging low, he looked so sad that none of Washakie's people came to greet him as they normally did.

They saw that something was wrong with Soaring Hawk and stepped aside, watching him silently as he walked on toward Chief Washakie's tepee. The chieftain's lodge was decorated with pictures of Washakie's exploits and victories of war, and his scalp pole stood at the right side of the entranceway, adorned with the scalps of those he had killed during his more youthful, warring days.

None of the scalps had belonged to the *tavois*, explorers and emigrants. Chief Washakie had only taken scalps from his red-skinned enemies.

As he drew near the chief's lodge, Soaring Hawk's attention was caught by a maiden who brushed past him and stopped breathlessly at Washakie's lodge before Soaring Hawk reached it.

He realized that the woman was unaware that Soaring Hawk was a stranger, that she took him for one of the warriors of her village. He realized now that no one had greeted him; there had been no indication that the village had a visitor.

He stepped aside, curious to see the profile of the young woman and was stunned by what he found. This was a white woman dressed to look like she was Shoshone.

Even more surprising was the effect she had on Soaring Hawk. He was awed by the woman's incredible beauty. Lovely and petite, she had the face of an angel, and he decided spontaneously that he would inquire of Washakie about her. He was so taken with her, it was as if someone had hit him with a fist in his belly, knocking the wind out of him.

Just as Misshi started to speak Washakie's name, she felt a presence behind her. She could feel eyes on her, devouring her, and she turned to see who was so interested in her.

Everyone in the village knew her well, so well they would not have to move closer to study her as she felt she was being studied now.

She swallowed hard, then turned slowly to see who was beside her. When she saw Soaring Hawk, she gasped and turned quickly back to Washakie's lodge.

Her heartbeats were like hammer blows inside her chest, for there, standing so close, was someone she had only been allowed to gaze upon from a

distance. She could not believe that the very man
of her dreams was standing there so close, the very
man she had secretly desired ever since she had
seen him five winters ago when he came for his
first council with Washakie.

She had been instantly attracted to his slender,
golden-bronze, muscular body, his high cheek-
bones, his lean, smooth features that reflected good
will and intelligence. His eyes were of the deepest
jet, his hair as lustrous as the raven's wing, falling
down his back.

As Soaring Hawk had sat inside the council
house with Washakie, Misshi had gone to one of
the warriors to inquire about the handsome young
brave.

She had discovered that his name was Soaring
Hawk and that he was a chief, a proud warrior who
had broken away from his marauding father's renegade band because he did not believe in his father's misguided ideals.

She had been stunned to discover that Soaring
Hawk was the son of the very man who had abducted her ten years ago. It was then that she had
discovered why she had been kept from Soaring
Hawk's sight. It was because of his relation to the
old, evil chief.

But it mattered not to her who his father was,

especially after learning he had separated himself from such a father.

She had fallen in love with Soaring Hawk the very first time she had seen him. He so handsome, so valorous, yet so forbidden to her.

But now that she was to choose a husband, would not it be wonderful to become acquainted with him . . . to become involved as man and woman?

Instead of hiding, she remained frozen to the spot as Soaring Hawk's eyes met and held hers.

"I know you," Misshi finally stammered out. "You . . . are . . . Soaring Hawk."

"*Huh*, I am Soaring Hawk," he said, noticing that her voice was soft, yet troubled. He did not want to believe that she was afraid of him.

"And you are . . . ?" Soaring Hawk asked, his pulse racing as he awaited the pleasure of her voice again.

But she looked like a rabbit that had been suddenly caught in a trap; words now seemed to fail her, and her beguiling violet eyes were wide, filled with an uneasiness that he wished she did not feel while in his presence.

Awed by Soaring Hawk's handsomeness, and remembering the dreams that she had had of him only last night, Misshi could not move, and she found she had suddenly lost her ability to speak.

Even when she heard footsteps behind her and the swish of buckskin as the entrance flap to Washakie's tepee was swept aside, even when Washakie was there beside her, Misshi could not will her feet to move, or her voice to speak.

Suddenly a gentle arm slid around Misshi's waist and Washakie's voice broke through the awkward silence. Unsure of how Washakie was going to react to this unplanned meeting, she turned slow eyes up to him.

Dressed in an elaborate robe made from skins of the bear, his long and flowing gray hair hanging down his back almost to the ground, Washakie ignored her. Instead, he focused his full attention on Soaring Hawk, and relief rushed through Misshi.

She turned and again gazed at Soaring Hawk, still astonished that she had finally met him.

"Welcome, Soaring Hawk," Washakie said. He reached a friendly hand out and placed it on Soaring Hawk's shoulder. "You have come unannounced today. There must be something of great importance to you to bring you to me so suddenly."

"My heart is burdened," Soaring Hawk said thickly. "You are always the one I bring my troubles to. Can I have counsel today?"

"Yes, always I am here to listen, in good times and bad," Washakie said. He dropped his hand down to his side. He took Misshi by the hand and

Savage Moon

turned her to face him. "My daughter, it seems you have come for counsel as well. Is that right?"

Misshi nodded.

"You were so anxious to see me that you were unaware of Soaring Hawk's presence in our village?" Washakie asked, his fathomless dark eyes gazing into Misshi's.

She nodded again, for words still eluded her.

Washakie turned again to Soaring Hawk. He smiled slowly. "It seems that fate today has arranged that you and my adopted daughter should finally meet," he said in his usual gentle, soothing voice. "Perhaps it is the will of the spirits. I am not one to argue with fate. Come, my children. Come into my lodge. We will share nourishment, then talk. If one of you chooses privacy for your personal counsel, so be it. But for now let us become as one in heart and voice."

Misshi was infinitely grateful for Washakie's wise ways. If he had scolded her and sent her to her lodge, forbidding her to meet Soaring Hawk, she was not sure she could have accepted his guidance.

Now that she had been so close to Soaring Hawk, had heard the magic of his voice, and seen the interest in his eyes, she could not turn away from him.

Happy that Washakie had not placed her in such a position, Misshi went inside the large tepee,

49

then turned and bashfully watched Soaring Hawk make his entrance with Chief Washakie.

When Soaring Hawk glanced her way and smiled, she felt a wonderful melting sensation.

Chapter Six

Love is . . . born with the pleasure
of looking at each other, it is fed
with the necessity of seeing each
other, it is concluded with the
impossibility of separation.

Jose Marti

Although Misshi had been in this lodge countless
times, she was always in awe of it. The tepee was
vast in size, as befitted a chief of Washakie's importance.

The tanned buffalo-skin wall of the tepee was
painted with battle scenes of Washakie's past. His
cache of weapons lay at one side of the lodge, his

bow worn from the many arrows that had been loosed from its string. His quiver of arrows, the buffalo skin stiff with age, hung from a pole that reached across the full length of the lodge. Washakie's war shield was positioned on a tripod just inside the entrance. It also showed signs of battle, with nicks gouged out of its tough leather exterior.

When Washakie motioned for Misshi to sit down on a blanket beside the lodge fire in the center of the tepee, she nodded, smiled, and hurried there. After lifting the hem of her fringed buckskin dress, she sank down onto the blanket and folded her legs beneath her.

Breathless with excitement over being in the same tepee as Soaring Hawk, Misshi watched as he was shown to a clean white pelt that had been spread opposite the fire from her.

Misshi was thankful that the fire burned low in the firepit, giving her a clear view of the handsome Bannock chief.

Through the years, she had always listened closely whenever his name was mentioned. She would hang on to each word, allowing those words to embrace her as though Soaring Hawk's powerful, muscled arms were actually enfolding her.

She blushed when she realized that he had caught her staring at him across the fire. His easy smile made her look away just as Washakie sat down on his plush pelts beside Soaring Hawk.

Enjoying her shyness, Soaring Hawk could not take his eyes off Misshi. He loved the way her black hair hung long down her back and framed her beautiful face.

Her violet eyes were mesmerizing, yet they made it obvious that she was not born Shoshone.

Everything else about her, however, *was* Shoshone: the way she dressed, her fondness and devotion to Washakie, her use of their language.

He wondered why she was living among the Shoshone, and why she had been kept a secret from him.

"Soaring Hawk," Washakie began, "there is a reason that I have never allowed my adopted daughter to be introduced to you." His dark eyes moved slowly to Misshi and he smiled. "You and I will speak later of why you came to my lodge with such excitement in your eyes, your excitement causing you to forget that you were not to be seen by Soaring Hawk."

Misshi wanted to explain that it was an accident, yet she knew it was not polite to interrupt Washakie.

Later there would be sufficient time to explain everything, especially her dreams, which had been filled with this Bannock chief.

She just smiled apologetically at Washakie, humbly lowering her eyes before looking up again as he addressed Soaring Hawk.

"Soaring Hawk, I will now tell you everything about my adopted daughter," Washakie said. "I will tell you how she came to be among my Shoshone people, and how it is that I think of her as a daughter, although I sent her to the dwelling of my widowed cousin for food, clothing, and lodging."

Soaring Hawk leaned slightly forward to hear the tale of this white woman who so fascinated him. Now that he had met her, there would be no keeping them apart.

The fact that she had been born white mattered not. In all ways that mattered, she was Indian!

"My son," Washakie began, addressing Soaring Hawk as "son" because he knew that Soaring Hawk thought of him as a father figure.

Forgetting his earlier fears that Soaring Hawk might tell his father about Misshi's presence among the Shoshone, Washakie told him everything: how he had found her wandering, and how she had escaped from Soaring Hawk's own father.

"It was my intention to find her brother and reunite the two, yet when a lengthy search proved fruitless, I allowed the young maiden to stay in my village, hoping to reunite her with her brother at a later date, or find a home for her with other white travelers who might want to take her in," Washakie said. "But as you see, she is still here. She is more Shoshone now than white. I have taken Misshi into my heart as though she were my own daughter."

The compliments and the depth of emotion with which Washakie spoke made Misshi want to go and hug him and tell him that she loved him just as much.

Yet she knew that it was not the right thing to do while someone was in Washakie's lodge for counsel.

Soaring Hawk gazed at Misshi. "It saddens me to know that my father brought such sorrow into your life," he said, his voice drawn. He smiled slowly. "Yet I am happy that your life has been so sweet among the Shoshone. But even though I know that you are happy, I still must apologize for the actions of Chief Bear. He is someone I am ashamed to call my father. It is with a sad heart that I must say I wish he was *not* my father, for he is a man hated by all who know him."

Soaring Hawk sighed heavily as he turned his eyes back to Washakie. "But it saddens me, as well, that you did not trust me enough to tell me about this maiden earlier," he said. "Why would you feel the need to keep her a secret from this warrior who is almost as a son to you?"

"I let no one but my people know about her. I feared that if somehow Chief Bear got this truth from you, he would come for her and demand her return. Soaring Hawk, Chief Bear *is* your father. Nothing can change that truth."

"Did you have so little faith in my friendship that you could not trust me?" Soaring Hawk said. "Does Washakie not know how much Soaring Hawk deplores his father's renegade ways? I would never wish to see a white woman held captive by my father."

Washakie's eyes wavered. "I humbly apologize," he said softly. "I was wrong to trust so little in a man who has been such a devoted friend to Washakie, a *son*. I hope that you can understand. Misshi is happy among my people. She is safe. She does not wish to live among the whites ever again."

"That is so," Misshi blurted out. "My place is here. My home is here. The Shoshone are my family now." She smiled sweetly at Washakie. "I love this man as much as I loved my very own father, God rest his soul." She lowered her eyes, then looked at Soaring Hawk again. "An arrow killed my father, but it was not shot by your father. He was killed on another day, during another raid."

"I can never make up to you what my father did that day, yet know that I would if I could," Soaring Hawk said softly. "It is good, though, that I see much happiness now in your eyes and hear it in your voice. One's life is so short compared with the life of mountains, rock, and wind. One must live one's life for today, as you have learned to live yours."

There was a pause; then Soaring Hawk motioned with a hand toward Misshi. "Your name," he said, an eyebrow lifting. "It is different, yet I am pleased by it."

She explained about how her brother had always lisped. "My true name is Mitzi," she murmured. "But I love the name Misshi. I would not want to be called anything else." She lowered her eyes and swallowed hard. "The name Misshi reminds me of my brother. It keeps my brother close to my heart."

She looked quickly up at Soaring Hawk. "Dale. Dale Bradley was his name," she said. Yet even if Dale was alive and came for her, she knew that she could not return to that way of life again. But it would be wonderful to know that he was alive.

"Why have you come today?" Misshi asked. "When you first arrived, you had such a forlorn look in your eyes. Why, Soaring Hawk? What has placed sadness in your heart and eyes?"

Washakie quickly intervened, drawing both Soaring Hawk and Misshi's eyes to him. "Soaring Hawk, please excuse this chief's ill manners. I should have asked why you came to the Shoshone village today," he said. "What is in your heart that made your shoulders and eyelids heavy when I first saw you?"

Soaring Hawk explained how his warrior had heard gossip at the trading post about Soaring Hawk's mother being ill.

"I am torn," Soaring Hawk concluded. "I wish to go and see her, yet I believe that if I did go to my father's village, he would not let me leave again alive. My father has been humiliated by my leaving to start a new life—a life that defies everything my father stands for."

Washakie leaned his head forward as he looked directly into Soaring Hawk's eyes. "My son, do you believe your mother is ill, or do you think this is a ploy by your father to entice you home?" he asked. "Do you even know where your father has established his new stronghold? You do know that your father changed the location of his stronghold after he learned of your departure."

Soaring Hawk momentarily hung his head, then gazed again at Washakie. "*Huh*, I, too, thought that my father might be using such a ploy," he said. "Do you truly believe Chief Bear would stoop so low to take his revenge that he would send false tales of his son's mother being ill?"

He had purposely ignored Washakie's question about whether he knew where his father now had his stronghold. Washakie was a dear friend, yet there were some things that Soaring Hawk shared with no one.

After searching for many months, Soaring Hawk *had* happened upon his father's stronghold. But he had shared the location with no one. As long as his mother was alive, as were so many other wives of the renegades, Soaring Hawk had not found it in himself to attack his father's stronghold.

But now he had no choice but to go up against his father. He hoped he could find a way to do it away from the stronghold. He wanted to spare the lives of the innocent women and children, if possible.

"I would not put anything past Chief Bear," Washakie said tightly. "He is a man of *che-kas-koi,* bad heart. His tactics, his evil, have worsened these past winters. It is as though a demon has been set free inside him."

He cleared his throat. "As far as your mother is concerned, if she *is* ill, or even dying, she would not want you risking your life to be with her. It would torment her, not help her, should your father take you captive upon your first arrival at his stronghold."

Soaring Hawk nodded. His mother would not want to be the cause of Soaring Hawk's captivity, or worse, his death.

"I must take my leave now," Soaring Hawk said. "I will go and pray, not only for my mother, but also for myself. I hurt inside to think she might be ill when I am so far away."

Soaring Hawk rose to his feet as did Washakie and Misshi. "Washakie, I want to thank you for your words of wisdom," he said as Washakie came to him with a warm embrace, which he returned.

"My son, come any time your heart is heavy and you have need of advice," Washakie said, stepping away from Soaring Hawk. He laughed softly as he gazed at Misshi. "But I cannot promise my adopted daughter's presence at the next council."

Soaring Hawk's lips curved into a soft smile. "It would be good if you could," he said, feeling warm inside when he saw how that statement made Misshi's eyes lower and her cheeks flush.

"Well, just perhaps something can be arranged," Washakie said as he took Soaring Hawk by an elbow and gently led him outside.

Misshi stepped out into the night behind them, where the moon had come up. She walked with Washakie and Soaring Hawk through the village to his horse.

Her eyes widened when Soaring Hawk stopped before mounting his strawberry roan and gazed seriously into Washakie's eyes.

"I would like your permission to come and see

Misshi again, and not only when she joins our council, but alone," he blurted out. "She is no longer a secret to me. I would like to know her better."

Misshi was stunned by the suddenness with which he announced his interest in her.

She thrilled inside when Washakie quickly agreed to Soaring Hawk's request.

Soaring Hawk and Washakie embraced one last time; then Soaring Hawk mounted his steed and rode away into the moonlit night.

Misshi clasped her hands together before her and watched Soaring Hawk until she could see him no longer.

She still couldn't believe that, finally, she was free not only to know Soaring Hawk, but actually to be with him . . . and love him!

Her dyed hair flying in the wind behind her, she squealed as she gave Washakie a quick hug, then hurried back into the village to tell her friends the exciting news about Soaring Hawk.

Washakie turned and watched her exuberance. He frowned. He had an uneasy feeling, now that Misshi's presence among his people had been discovered.

He turned and walked slowly back into his village.

Chapter Seven

Happy, thrice happy and more,
are they whom an unbroken bond
Unites and whose love shall know
no sundering quarrels,
so long as they shall live.
—Horace

The moon's glow shone down through the smoke
hole, mingling with the slowly rising smoke from
the firepit below, creating slowly dancing, ghostly
apparitions.

Sitting on thick pelts beside the fire in Chief
Bear's massive tepee, White Snow Feather softly
caressed her husband's brow with a damp buckskin

cloth as he lay motionless beside her, his eyes watching the flames lick the half-burned logs in the firepit.

Dressed in a beautifully beaded white doeskin dress, her graying hair hanging in one thick, long braid down her back, White Snow Feather glared up at Panther Eyes as he paced back and forth across the bulrush mats opposite the fire.

As Panther Eyes continued to pace nervously, like a panther waiting for its prey to come closer so that it could pounce, White Snow Feather's resentment of this man grew stronger by the moment.

Ah, yes, she did resent him, for Panther Eyes, who had always been Chief Bear's right-hand man, was now in charge of Bear's stronghold. He had taken over since Chief Bear had been injured that day some years back when a bullet had entered his skull.

The bullet had not been a fatal one, but it had rendered Bear feeble-minded. He could no longer be his people's leader.

A strong, determined man, with the same ferocious ideals as his downed chief, Panther Eyes had taken charge. It was he who led the vicious raids now, not Bear.

But, White Snow Feather thought to herself, Panther Eyes always made sure that when whites

Savage Moon

or enemy redskins died, it was Bear who was given the credit for the heinous acts against humanity.

It hurt White Snow Feather to know that her husband was talked about as though he were the white man's devil for things he was no longer responsible for.

The peaceful tribes of Indians, and the white soldiers and settlers who were trying to work together to establish harmony, were all plotting against White Snow Feather's husband, not knowing that he no longer deserved their hatred.

If she had her way, she would leave this stronghold with her husband and let those who hated him see that he was now a man who knew not one sunset from another. Surely his enemies would take pity on him and allow White Snow Feather to live a normal life with Bear far from this place she now hated with all of her being.

But Panther Eyes had made sure that was not possible. She was a prisoner now in her own home. She was not free to travel beyond the boundaries of the stronghold.

She detested Panther Eyes for keeping her captive and hoped that one day soon someone would do away with him. She smiled as she thought of his scalp swaying on someone's scalp pole.

But until that day she had no choice but to stay where she was and care for her invalid husband, for he was her life. Her son had been gone now for many winters, but she did not resent his absence. She gloried in it, for her son was making something good of his life.

"I cannot understand a son who would not come to the sickbed of his ailing mother," Panther Eyes grumbled as he stopped and knelt on the other side of the fire. He glared at her through the thin patch of smoke. "Your son loves you so little, he cares not about your welfare. How does that make you feel?"

He chuckled beneath his breath, then said, "Do you hate him now as much as you hate Panther Eyes?"

"My son loves me too much to come, for he is astute enough to know that tales of my illness are false," White Snow Feather said in a low hiss. "He knows that it would kill me to see him die at the hands of such a man as you."

She laughed cynically. "But as I said, my son is too astute to take such bait that you have laid out for him. He is a man who prays and whose prayers are answered. In his prayers he sees his mother well and strong."

She looked slowly down at her husband, stiffening inside when she saw drool streaming from one corner of his mouth.

She quickly placed the soft buckskin cloth there and gently wiped the drool away.

She laid the cloth in a wooden bowl of water and again glared at Panther Eyes. "My son Soaring Hawk will one day even see you in his prayers. He will see how you are wronging his mother, how you are keeping me prisoner in this lodge with my ailing husband," she said, her voice breaking.

Again she laughed mockingly. "And do not think he did not come because he was not smart enough to search out and find this stronghold that you established far away from the one in which he was born," she said bitterly. "Soaring Hawk knows, Panther Eyes. In time, he will make his move, and you will see just how his intelligence outdoes yours. Then you will die, Panther Eyes. You . . . will . . . die."

"When I die, so will you," Panther Eyes said. He spit toward her, his spittle landing just short of her in a sizzling hiss in the flames of the fire.

He gazed at his chief, his eyes only then growing softer. He felt an affection that would never die for this man who had made Panther Eyes his special friend, his right-hand man in all raids and battles.

"Sadly, then too will my chief die," he said.

"Your devotion to my husband is not something honorable," White Snow Feather said icily. "If he

67

knew how you treated me, you would see just how quickly he would send a knife into your heart. I would laugh as you lay there writhing before you died."

She laughed again. "But as it is, Panther Eyes, it will be my *son* who will destroy you," she said. "In time, Panther Eyes. In time, you will see. Yes, you will see."

"Hush, woman," Panther Eyes said as he leaped to his feet. He doubled his hands into tight fists at his sides. "One day you will say too much and I will forget you are the wife of my chief. It would please me so much to silence your words forever, for I am sorely tired of not only your words, but your voice. It irritates me so much, sometimes I want to cry to the heavens for a lightning bolt to strike you dead and silence your voice forever."

"I would even welcome that lightning bolt, if it meant escape from this wretched life," White Snow Feather said. She reached a hand to her husband's brow, slowly caressing the leathery skin. "But only if Bear came with me. In the other life, where all of our ancestors roam, he would be well again, he would know me. We would be young lovers again, as we were before the deaths of his parents changed him—"

"Hush, woman," Panther said, interrupting her.

"If your son had his way, what you pray for would come to pass sooner than you think."

He bent to a knee and glared through the smoke at her again. "News has come to Panther Eyes that Soaring Hawk has plans to kill his chieftain father and all who are under his leadership," he said. "Your son does not know that it is Panther Eyes he should be hunting, not a chief who no longer even knows his own name. But believe me when I say that no one will stop me, especially not Soaring Hawk. I want to spill blood across this land until the rivers run red with it. Then maybe whites will stop invading the hunting grounds that once belonged solely to the red man."

As White Snow Feather listened, her heart grew colder and colder, for she knew that Panther Eyes would stop at nothing to lure her son into his clutches.

She had never before felt so helpless, for she knew that there was nothing she could do to stop this madman from plotting against her son or the rest of mankind.

It made her insides ache to know that it was her very own husband who had started these killings and maimings, who had taught Panther Eyes his evil ways.

Out of devotion to Bear, White Snow Feather had stayed with her husband. On the day of her son's escape, she had hoped to have a long talk with her husband, to make him see the wrong in his actions . . . a wrong that had driven his son from him.

But a bullet had changed all of that. Her plans to alter her life, as well as her husband's, had come too late.

But her son had won his freedom and led the kind of life that she had hoped for from the day he was born.

"Although my plan to lure your son to the stronghold has failed, he will come one day, for if he is so determined to stop his father, he *will* find this stronghold," Panther Eyes said, a slow, evil smile on his lips.

With a growl he stood up. He clasped his hands together behind his back and stared into the dancing flames of the fire. "I had hoped that if he thought you were ill, he would come alone to be with you. I had planned that while he was here, without the aid of his warriors, I would end his life."

"Yes, you are the sort who *would* kill your chief's son while he is among his own people," White Snow Feather said. "Panther Eyes, hear me well when I say that if I were able to come and go as I please, I would have stopped your meanness long ago. You, who have been even more vicious than my husband ever was, have dirtied his name so much that even his son now feels the need to kill him. Ah, yes, if I were not held hostage in my own lodge among my own people, I would have found a way to prove that it is you, not my husband, who is now spilling so much blood in Wyoming land."

"Watch what you say, woman, or I shall cut the tongue from your mouth," Panther Eyes said, again bending to his haunches so that his eyes were level with White Snow Feather's. "I will forget that you are my chief's wife. My life would be better without you."

"Say what you will against me, for I am already dead inside my heart," White Snow Feather said, her voice filled with sadness. "A part of my heart does wish that Soaring Hawk had found the stronghold and come. Finally he would know that it is not his father who kills so heartlessly—that his father passes his days smiling peacefully, unaware of the evil that surrounds him in his own village. Threaten me with words as often as you wish, Panther Eyes, for it matters not to me. Had I not been a prisoner in my own village, I would have reunited father and son, for Soaring Hawk would not abandon a father who has no ability to even think anymore, much less kill. The bullet rendered him helpless long ago."

"You say that my threats fall on deaf ears?" Panther Eyes said, chuckling. "If you do not stop talking, I will kill you and finally silence your tongue. No one would even suspect that I did it. As far as anyone knows, we are allies in crime. No one knows that you do not leave your lodge because I have said that is the way it should be. All think you stay hidden away because of your devotion to your husband. You have known that to tell your true feelings to our people would be to make your mindless husband a widower. Who then would pamper him? Who, White Snow Feather? Who then would wipe the drool from your husband's mouth?"

Knowing that his words were true, and fearing that she might have said too much today, she decided to back down.

As she spoke a humble apology, Panther Eyes' maniacal laughter filled her veins with cold loathing.

Chapter Eight

Our passions are most like to floods and streams
The shallow murmur, but the deep are dumb.
—Sir Walter Raleigh
"Sir Walter Raleigh to the Queen" (1599)

Daylight was just breaking along the horizon when several soldiers dressed as Indians rode through the open gates of Fort Adams.

Dale Bradley, now a cavalryman, a major, was in the lead.

He nodded a silent command to those who followed, sending them to their quarters.

They had baths to take, for most had blood spattered on their breechclouts and bodies. They had dressed as Indians so that redskins, not white soldiers, would be blamed for their acts.

As Dale went his own way, toward the colonel's quarters where he now made his residence, he smiled crookedly.

Yes, tonight he and his men had made a successful silent attack on a sleeping village of Shoshone.

As he had ripped open one tepee after another with his sharp knife, he had thought of Misshi. He was doing this killing to avenge her.

Yes, tonight he had had his little sister's face in his mind's eye when he had killed women, men, and children in their sleep.

He had laughed mockingly when he took the Indians' scalps and weapons.

He had purposely not taken horses, because to have them in his possession would be proof of who had committed the slaughter tonight—he and his men!

Instead, they'd freed the animals from their corrals and scattered them.

When Dale reached his quarters, he dismounted and tied his stallion's reins to a hitching rail. Proud of what he had achieved tonight, he grabbed the leather bag that held his prize scalps.

He slung the bag over his shoulder, then reached for another bag which held tomahawks, knives, and even arrows that he had taken from the tepees. He collected weapons, but his real pleasure lay in the scalps he'd taken, both from the dead and from the scalp poles in the tepees.

They were *his* trophies now.

He was so glad that he had never found any with the exact reddish-golden color of his sister's hair.

"I have given up on ever seeing Misshi again," he mumbled to himself as he went inside his cabin, where he had left kerosene lanterns burning for his return home. "But as long as I live, I shall continue to look for her, and to listen for talk of a white woman living among redskins."

He lumbered into his office at the front of the cabin and tossed his bags on the floor, then fell to his knees and carefully pried up a loose floor board.

As the lantern's glow lit his secret cache, Dale chuckled and a wicked glint appeared in his eyes. He stared down at guns, scalps, bows and arrows, and Indian jewelry, all taken during his raids on innocent Indians.

Yes, he had many trophies. He now dumped everything he had gotten tonight into the open space.

"Sis, it's all for you," he said and slowly replaced the board, blocking the smell of fresh blood from the new scalps added to his collection.

Tired, he went to his bedroom at the back of

the cabin. He dropped the breechclout, then sat down on his bed and yanked off the moccasins.

He rose from the bed, pulled off the black wig that he always wore to disguise himself as an Indian, then went nude to a washbasin that he had filled with water before leaving earlier with his men. He was always anxious to remove the stench of redskins from his flesh.

As he leaned low over the basin and began splashing himself with water, then picked up a bar of soap and scrubbed his freckled flesh, he became lost in thought.

He had gone to the Missouri River with the survivors of the Indian ambush that day his sister was abducted. There he had boarded a paddlewheeler, which took him far from this land he now detested.

After he arrived in Kansas City, Missouri, he had tried to settle into a regular sort of life. He had married the first woman who lifted her skirts to him, enraptured by the glimpse of paradise she had shown him.

Having a woman in his bed each night had helped get his mind off the loss of his entire family on that fateful journey from Ohio. But it didn't take long for Dale to realize that his wife, Sally, wasn't giving herself only to him. She had lied to another man and had exchanged vows with him as well. After investigating the matter, Dale was stunned to learn that his Sally belonged to not one, but three other men!

When he confronted her with the truth, she laughingly bragged about all of the money she had in a bank vault, money she had accumulated from the expensive gifts given to her by her "husbands," and from stealing money out of their pockets while they were asleep. Furious, Dale had physically lifted her from the floor and thrown her out the door of his home.

He had stood there laughing at her as she lay in a puddle of mud, a look of bewilderment on her face that any man would treat her in such a callous way. Then he slammed the door on her and the marriage, and joined the cavalry.

He continued thinking about his past as he dried himself with a towel, then slid down onto his bed, nude, and lay on his back staring out a window at the star-speckled sky.

Yes, he thought to himself, he had been a cavalryman for many years now.

Although he did not have the title of colonel yet, he had fooled those in charge of the cavalry into liking and trusting him enough that he had been asked to take over the reins of this new fort in Wyoming after the colonel in charge, a Frank Adams, had been killed.

Everyone thought that Indians had killed Colonel Adams.

But they were wrong. It had been Dale who had schemed and killed the colonel in order to carry out his plan of avenging his sister's abduction without interference.

To make Washington truly believe that he was devoted to the dead colonel, Dale had suggested that they name the newly established fort in honor of Colonel Adams. Thus Fort Adams had been established, as had Dale's leadership there until another colonel arrived.

Dale hoped he would now have enough time to kill many redskins before his replacement arrived, for that was his sole reason for joining the cavalry in the first place.

But there was one Indian in particular that he'd been warned never to harm.

"Chief Washakie," Dale said, sitting up and pulling on a robe.

He left the bed and grabbed up his pipe. He took it out to the front room of the cabin and sat down in a rocking chair, lighting the pipe from the glimmering orange remains of the fire he had built just prior to going on the raid.

As he sucked on the stem of his pipe and rocked slowly back and forth, he thought more about this chief called Washakie. He had to be careful not to step over the line and go after that Indian. Colonel Harry Braddock, who was in charge of the cavalry at nearby Fort Bridger, was known to be a close friend of Chief Washakie.

Thus far, Dale had been able to obey the order about Washakie, for there were many other redskins to kill.

"But there'll be no stopping me when I find Chief Bear's stronghold," Dale grumbled to himself.

Yes, he planned to wipe the entire stronghold off the face of the earth, but first he had to find it. He knew it couldn't be far away, for Chief Bear and his renegade warriors were responsible for many deadly raids in this area.

"I will not rest until I kill the chief who took my sister away," he said out loud.

And if he ever saw him, ah, yes, he would know him. Who could forget that scarred face and the one drooping eye?

Vengeance for Misshi's sake was now Dale's only reason for living. He would never trust any woman again enough to marry her.

He planned to use all of his energy finding Misshi and killing off as many redskins as possible while he continued to search for her.

If his sister was still alive, surely he would find her one day. He was not far now from the place where his sister had been taken from him.

"Tomorrow," he said, chuckling.

Yes, tomorrow he planned to attack a wagon train. But as he had done before, he would make it look like an Indian ambush. That was a must.

He wanted Colonel Harry Braddock at Fort Bridger to believe that the Indians in this area were on the warpath. He wanted Colonel Braddock to be put in the position of having to decide to go to war with the Indians.

Dale knew that if that happened, the army would send enough cavalrymen to finally rid the area of all renegades. Chief Bear's stronghold would be uncovered in the process.

Chief Bear would finally die.

"My sister's abduction, and possible death, will finally be avenged," he said, a hint of madness in his green eyes as he laughed menacingly.

His laughter faded into a low growl as he thought further of Chief Bear's stronghold. He thought he had found clues to the whereabouts of the old renegade's hideout.

He was eager to see if his suspicions were correct. If they were, he would get the full honor of taking the old chief in alive or dead, and he would finally learn whether Misshi was there.

Once Chief Bear was taken care of, Dale's vengeance would be achieved. He would be ready to leave the cavalry and try his hand at another career.

Of late, he had discovered he had a talent for singing. He couldn't help wondering how it would feel to perform before an audience in St. Louis's beautiful opera house.

He chuckled as he stretched out on his back.

"Yeah, why not?" he whispered.

But first things first. He had to see to Chief Bear's demise, and learn whether his sister might be alive.

If he didn't discover answers about Misshi now, he never would.

Chapter Nine

Love conquers all things;
let us, too, surrender to love.
—Virgil

Soaring Hawk stood on a bluff near his stronghold as he watched a warrior make his way down the narrow pass to return to Washakie's village.

This scout, who was called Black Bull, had brought sad tidings today to Soaring Hawk from Washakie. There had been another atrocity committed against a band of Washakie's Shoshone tribe.

All had been slaughtered in their sleep. Women, men, children, and elderly alike had fallen victim to the same group that had been wreaking murder and mayhem across this beautiful Wyoming land.

It did not seem to make any difference whether those slaughtered were red-skinned or white. It seemed that some madman enjoyed the sight of blood so much, he could not get enough of killing.

And last night, while the moon was still high in the sky and bright, the killers had gone on one of their murdering sprees. They not only murdered, but also took scalps from those they attacked, as well as weapons and valuables.

It puzzled Soaring Hawk why they had taken no horses.

Black Bull had said that the horses had been scattered in all different directions.

"That had to have been done to confuse those who would want to avenge this latest atrocity," Soaring Hawk whispered, his eyes still watching Black Bull make the treacherous trek down the winding, steep path that led from Soaring Hawk's stronghold.

As Black Bull had described the kill, it pointed to Soaring Hawk's father and his renegade warriors. Those who had died had been silently killed by arrows, knives, and hatchets so that the murders could be done without awakening any warriors who would stop them.

Savage Moon

And the scalps had been removed with the skill of one who did this often.

Soaring Hawk grimaced and squeezed his eyes tightly closed in an attempt not to picture the many scalps on his father's scalp pole. He tried not to remember the stench of the scalps, which had sent his stomach reeling the first time he had smelled them.

He knew then, even before his mother began teaching him how to walk a vastly different path from his father, that he would never take anyone's scalp.

It was a horrendous practice, yet many looked upon it as an act of valor.

It desperately saddened him to believe that this latest atrocity could be the work of his father. Chief Washakie knew that Soaring Hawk would be more determined than ever now to find and stop Chief Bear.

Washakie had invited Soaring Hawk to come to his village this evening to join Washakie's people in two rituals, the Wolf Dance and the Ghost Dance. The purpose of the latter was to drive out the ghost, or evil spirit, that had brought death to Washakie's Shoshone tribe.

Washakie hoped that the Ghost Dance ritual would slow down Chief Bear's evil enough to give Washakie's and Soaring Hawk's warriors time to

85

find their enemy's stronghold before he did any more killing.

Soaring Hawk realized now that he must tell Chief Washakie he already knew where his father's stronghold was. He had already sent word back to Washakie by way of Black Bull that he would come tonight to plan Chief Bear's downfall.

He had already readied his horse for travel to Washakie's village and dressed himself in special attire for the occasion. He wore a shirt and leggings made of clean white dressed deerskin, with black stripes painted around the arms and legs, and fringed with ermine skins. He also wore a necklace made of the claws of the grizzly bear, worked into a strip of otter skin.

He wondered if his dress would impress Misshi.

He smiled to himself, thinking it did not seem she needed any more impressing. He was sure she had feelings for him, and that knowledge made his loins ache with need of her.

Having explained to his people where he was going, Soaring Hawk mounted his steed and began his slow journey down the mountainside.

He had purposely sent Black Bull on ahead, for Soaring Hawk's heart was too heavy to join in idle conversation with anyone on this journey. He wanted to spend time on his steed alone today.

As tiny pebbles and rocks were dislodged by his

horse's hooves, Soaring Hawk made his way down the narrow, steep path. He wondered if Washakie would allow Misshi to join them tonight during the ceremony.

Surely now that Misshi and Soaring Hawk had met, Washakie would not make her go into hiding again.

Soaring Hawk hoped he would soon be able to tell his own people about her, secret from even *his* people, for he wanted her with him always!

He had finally found a woman he could envision sitting with him beside his nightly lodge fire. He could envision her lying in bed with him, beneath his blankets. He had even gone as far as envisioning her holding their first-born child in her arms as it fed at her milk-filled breast.

His thoughts of Misshi kept him so engrossed that suddenly he found himself entering the outer perimeters of Washakie's village.

He dismounted near Washakie's lodge, handed his reins to a young brave who took his steed to the corral, then smiled at Washakie as he stepped from his lodge.

Washakie put his left arm over Soaring Hawk's right shoulder, clasping his back while pressing his left cheek to Soaring Hawk's and saying, "*Ah-hi-e, ah-hi-e,*" in the Shoshone way of showing pleasure.

Soaring Hawk returned the same embrace and

greeted Washakie with the same words; then the two friends eased apart.

"*Keemah,* come. Come inside my lodge for private time before we go to the large council house for the ceremony," Washakie said as he swept the entranceway flap aside for Soaring Hawk.

Washakie was dressed appropriately for tonight's ceremonies. He wore a buffalo robe adorned with beads and porcupine quills and a colorful blanket slung across his left shoulder.

As soon as he entered Washakie's lodge, Soaring Hawk was keenly aware of Misshi sitting beside Washakie's lodge fire on snow white pelts, all decked out and beautiful in her white, heavily beaded attire, with vermilion—signifying peace and harmony—lightly applied to her lovely pink face.

"Sit," Washakie said as he gestured toward a bear pelt not far from where Misshi sat. He then seated himself beside Soaring Hawk.

"I have asked you to my village tonight," Washakie said, "not only for the Wolf and Ghost Dance and talk of hunting down a killer, but also to tell you that it is time for Misshi, my daughter, to take a husband." Washakie's dark eyes gleamed as he gazed into Soaring Hawk's.

Misshi's insides quivered with excitement as Washakie spoke. She had known ever since daybreak this morning of her chief's plan to bring Soaring Hawk into his private lodge tonight before the Wolf and Ghost Dance rituals. She had almost become sick from excitement as she awaited this moment. Now she leaned forward and scarcely breathed, gazing at Soaring Hawk while awaiting his reaction to Washakie's request.

Soaring Hawk's heart was hammering like a sledge hammer inside his chest, for even before Washakie finished what he was saying, he knew that Washakie was including Soaring Hawk in Misshi's future.

"It would honor Washakie and his entire village if Soaring Hawk would consider taking Misshi as his wife," Washakie said.

Washakie slid a slow smile over at Misshi, then smiled at Soaring Hawk. "Misshi has spoken favorably of you," he said. "Soaring Hawk, how do you feel about what I have just asked of you? Is it not time for your blankets to be warmed by a woman's body? Does not Misshi stir your loins?"

A quick rush of heat rose to Misshi's cheeks, and she gasped, embarrassed by Washakie's openness in speaking about Soaring Hawk's loins!

Her face hot with a blush, she quickly lowered her eyes.

Soaring Hawk, too, was taken aback by Washakie's frank words, but had that not always been the way between Soaring Hawk and Washakie? Open, honest, and leaving nothing unsaid between them?

Except for one thing, yes, Soaring Hawk had been totally open with this older statesman. Only the location of his father's stronghold had he kept hidden. But he would soon reveal it, when the time came to speak of such things again.

First, however, more important subjects were being discussed.

Misshi!

He could hardly believe that Washakie had intuited Soaring Hawk's deep feelings for Misshi without his ever sharing them with the Shoshone chief.

Soaring Hawk's loins *were* on fire. His heartbeats were so rapid it was as though drums were pounding in his ears, thumping . . . thumping . . . thumping.

He looked quickly at Washakie. "*Huh*, it *is* time for me to have a woman share my bed . . . and all that I have," he said. "And I am honored from the depths of my heart that you, my dear friend Washakie, have chosen me to be Misshi's husband. I will gladly court her. I will be good to her. I will make you glad that you have chosen me to wed her."

Washakie nodded, yet in his heart he was not

completely comfortable with what he had done. Yes, he had decided that Soaring Hawk was right for Misshi, and had approached Soaring Hawk because he felt guilty for doubting him in any respect.

Yet still, there it was! That nagging doubt!

His expression was serious as he gazed intently into Soaring Hawk's eyes. "Soaring Hawk, does it matter to you that Misshi is white . . . that in truth she belongs to your father because it was he who took her as his prize . . . his spoils of war?" he asked guardedly. "Would you feel as though you were being disloyal to your father by taking the property he must still believe is his?"

There was a strained silence in the tepee.

Then, shocked and angry at Washakie for the first time since he had taken her, Misshi rose to her feet. With her hands knotted into tight fists at her sides, she stared disbelievingly down at Washakie.

"Taking someone by force does not make a person one's property," she said, her voice drawn. "You surely do not believe that. You know that I no longer feel white. I am Shoshone, through and through. Even if I should come face to face with my true blood-brother, Dale, I would not want to be reunited with him and live the life of a white person again. I love the Shoshone. I love you, Washakie, no less than if you were my true father."

91

A sob escaped her. "Washakie, do you not love me as much?"

Washakie hurried to his feet.

He rushed to Misshi and drew her into his arms. "I am sorry if I have said things that hurt you," he said thickly. "Of course I no longer see you as white. I do not see you as anyone's property. I see you as my lovely daughter, whom I wish to see wed to a man of good heart like Soaring Hawk."

She clung to him for a moment longer, then eased from his arms and gazed smilingly up at him. "I am sorry if I reacted too quickly to what you said," she murmured. "I should have known that it was not said to hurt me or Soaring Hawk."

"No, I wish only to spare you hurt," Washakie said, placing a gentle hand on her cheek.

Then he drew her to his side and held her there as he gazed down at Soaring Hawk. "Stand before me, my son, so that we can look eye to eye when I apologize to you," he said, his voice drawn.

Soaring Hawk rose to his feet and faced Washakie.

"Soaring Hawk, you do not have to respond to what I said about Chief Bear," he said, resting his hand on Soaring Hawk's muscled shoulder. "I know your true feelings about your father. I see no loyalty to him when I look into your eyes and heart. And that is good, for that man deserves no loyalty from such a son as you whose life is guided by goodness, not evil."

Soaring Hawk smiled and nodded. "I understand why you felt the need to say what you said, and I have no ill feelings about it, for were my father different, I *would* feel loyalty toward him," he said. "You felt the need to test me. Know that I feel my father deserves no loyalty."

"In every sense, you are *my* son," Washakie said softly. "And you will truly be my son after your marriage to my daughter."

Misshi thrilled inside to know that this was really happening. She would be wife to such a man as Soaring Hawk. She felt as though she were soaring in the clouds.

Soaring Hawk gazed at Misshi and could almost read her heart, know what she was thinking as she smiled at him. He was feeling the same thrill to know that soon she would be his.

They would be man and wife!

"*Keemah*, come. Let us join the others in the council house," Washakie said. He stepped aside so that Soaring Hawk could move up beside Misshi.

He smiled proudly as Soaring Hawk took Misshi's hand and led her outside the teepee, where the moon was spreading its brilliant white light over the whole village.

* * *

Not far away from the Shoshone village a group of travelers were sitting around a campfire, their covered wagons in a protective circle around them. The air was sweet with the smell of cooked rabbit and coffee brewing on the coals of the fire.

But nearby, glittering, evil green eyes watched them from high above, soon to make a beautiful moon become suddenly . . . savage.

Chapter Ten

O time, arrest your flight! and you,
  propitious hours, arrest your
Course! Let us savor the fleeting
  delights of our most beautiful days!
      —Alphonse de Lamartini

In the council house everyone was seated around the great fire on green boughs covered with antelope skins.

Misshi sat entranced not by the actual ritual being performed before her, for she had seen it many times, but by the man who sat at her side.

Should anyone have told her only two days ago that she would be in the company of Soaring

Hawk, or that he would accept Washakie's offer to make Misshi his wife, she would have laughed and said it was impossible.

But it was all real enough, and she understood the haste with which this was occurring. She had seen it many times before.

In these parts, life could be snuffed out so quickly by crazed renegades, or even by quirks of nature such as floods, lightning strikes, and sudden rockfalls.

Because life could be harsh here in Wyoming land, a person did not wait long to marry once love struck.

She was so happy that the man she adored felt the same about her as she did about him, and that they could begin planning a future together. She prayed that nothing would stand in the way of their plans to marry.

Her mind was brought back to the ceremony at hand as she watched the last of the dancing in the council house. The Wolf Dance was coming to an end.

Only the men of the village had taken part in it. They were decked out in brilliant colored feathers and wore elaborate paint on their faces and powder in their hair.

In this round dance the warriors had appealed to the "Great Wolf Mystery" for success in their undertakings and prayed that they might overcome their enemies. The most gifted of the dancers were believed to be able to attack an enemy in the dark, because of their special ability to see the footprints of the wolf illuminated.

Next the dancers performed the Ghost Dance.

Misshi knew that some Indians participated in the Ghost Dance for five days and nights until the dancers fell to the earthen floor with exhaustion. She was glad that the performances and prayers would be for only this one night, for if it were not so, her marriage to Soaring Hawk would be delayed far longer than she wished.

As it was, she would have to wait until Washakie and Soaring Hawk's attack on Chief Bear had been completed. It might take days, possibly weeks, just to find the location of his stronghold.

She was not sure if she could bear such a long wait as that, yet had she not waited years to meet the man of her dreams? She could be patient a little while longer.

She almost swooned on the spot when Soaring Hawk suddenly moved closer to her and their shoulders touched. He no longer held her hand, for it had drawn much attention when they had entered the lodge hand-in-hand.

The time would come for everyone to understand the depth of their feelings for one another.

97

But for now only she, Soaring Hawk, and Washakie knew what the future would hold for Soaring Hawk and Misshi.

She tried to focus on the dancers, for she knew that soon they would seat themselves, and their chief could stand to say a prayer that would end the ceremony.

Many of Washakie's warriors, who were dressed in ermine-trimmed breechclouts and moccasins, each with a blanket thrown across his right shoulder, had formed a circle at the beginning of the dance. There were so many dancers tonight that a larger circle than usual had been formed around the fire. Standing between each man was a woman dressed in beautifully beaded doeskin and moccasins.

There was no instrumental accompaniment to the Ghost Dance, but the dancers sang as they held hands and shuffled their feet sideways, moving constantly to the left.

Misshi realized the dance was now almost over. She knew this because the hands of the men and women were falling free from one another and the men were reaching for the blankets on their shoulders.

Suddenly the dancers stopped. The women moved back from the men.

The council house was filled with a hushed silence as each warrior began shaking his blanket with one hand, while his other hand pounded his breast. The men chanted loudly as they looked heavenward through the smoke hole overhead.

Suddenly the chanting stopped, the blankets were stilled, and the warriors stepped away from the circle, joining the women as they took their places on the bough-covered floor.

Chief Washakie rose to his feet and moved into the circle of his people. He was met with looks of adoration, for this chief was both trusted and revered.

For a moment Washakie stood there, looking from person to person. Then he turned his hands and his eyes heavenward and began praying.

"Spirits of my people's dead relatives, I make this prayer to you," he cried. "I call on all the spirits of our dead friends to aid in giving us what we ask for tonight. Help us to rid this land of the evil of those who kill needlessly. I make this prayer to you so that our children will live a long life and so that our elders will still be able to sit peacefully by the fire and smoke as they reminisce of times long past. I call on all you spirits and ask you to assist in helping the warriors who will go soon to fight for the sake of our people. So be it!"

Everyone joined in with the same words. "So be it!"

And then the lodge was filled with the voices and laughter of the people as they rose to their feet and began filing from the lodge.

Misshi left the council house with Soaring Hawk to her left, Washakie to her right.

When they reached Washakie's tepee, he turned and faced Misshi and Soaring Hawk. "I know that you want to be alone," he said. "Go now. Have your walk. I will sit by my fire and think of what lies ahead. I must pray more for guidance."

"You won't be leaving to search for Bear's stronghold as early as tomorrow, will you?" Misshi asked. She wanted at least one full day with Soaring Hawk before bidding him farewell for many days, perhaps weeks.

"This is not something that should be done in haste, yet I do not plan to wait much longer," Washakie said, reaching for Misshi. He gently hugged her, then stepped away from her and looked from her to Soaring Hawk. "I feel we must first meet with Colonel Braddock at Fort Bridger to let him know what we plan to do. It is always best to include Colonel Braddock in such a scheme as this. Tomorrow I will send our scout ahead to inform him of our visit. Soaring Hawk, does that suit you?"

"Your decisions are always wise, and, yes, I will proceed with this as you plan it," Soaring Hawk said, wondering if this was the time to reveal the location of his father's stronghold.

But knowing that Washakie was bringing Colonel Braddock into the plan, it seemed even more important to keep the knowledge of his father's stronghold to himself. He would not want the colonel to put Washakie in the position of being forced to tell where the stronghold was. Soaring Hawk wanted no cavalrymen to have the opportunity to go to his father's stronghold before Soaring Hawk and Washakie went themselves.

Soaring Hawk wanted to be there when his father was captured, or killed.

He wanted the opportunity to ensure that his mother didn't die in the fracas.

"Go. Enjoy the moon and stars," Washakie said, smiling from Misshi to Soaring Hawk. Then he grew somber again as he reached a hand to Soaring Hawk's shoulder. "It will be good to have you as my son by marriage. I wish that I had not kept my daughter from you. It was wrong."

"But I know her now," Soaring Hawk said, sliding a slow smile over at Misshi. "And already it is as though I have known her forever. In a sense, I have. I knew deep inside my heart that she was there for me. I just had to wait for the right time to meet her."

Cassie Edwards

Soaring Hawk hugged Washakie and watched with Misshi as he entered his lodge.

Then, feeling full of irrepressible joy, Misshi laughed and began running toward the beckoning darkness of the forest.

"*Mea*, come!" she cried. "It is finally our time alone together! I do not want to waste another moment of this beautiful moonlit night!"

Soaring Hawk's heart swelled with joy as he stood there a moment longer just watching her. Ah, she was such a sight to behold, this woman who was now his.

Small and graceful, she ran like a deer, her long black hair streaming behind her in the breeze. Her laughter was as sweet as bird song. To Soaring Hawk, she was a miracle . . . someone surely sent from heaven.

He laughed into the wind as he began running after her. When they came to the water's edge some distance from Washakie's village, where a bluff made a ragged shadow over the embankment, Soaring Hawk reached for Misshi's hand and stopped her.

As she turned to him, her eyes filled with dancing moonbeams, she felt as though she would melt when she saw the way he was looking at her.

She felt weak in the knees when he took her

into his arms and his lips met hers in a sweet, joyous kiss.

She clung to him as she returned the kiss, for
although she was admired by many warriors, she
had not been kissed by any of them. And, ah, this
kiss! How could she have ever imagined it could
be this perfect . . . this luscious?

His lips pressed against hers, so warm, so true.
His body, too, was molded against hers, making the
world a much different place for Misshi than it had
been before this moment.

Soaring Hawk was aware that too much was
happening too soon. The heat in his loins had built
to something almost unbearable, a heat that could
only be quelled by taking Misshi to bed and making love with her. He paid heed to the warnings
and eased her from his arms.

They stood for a moment longer gazing into one
another's eyes, as Misshi struggled with the feelings
that had overwhelmed her as their kisses had deepened and their bodies had begun to strain so hun-
grily together.

She knew that it was right to stop now. Their
restraint would make their future time together as
lovers even more precious.

She was so glad that Soaring Hawk put his respect for her ahead of the needs of his body.

"Let us just sit and talk tonight," Soaring Hawk said, his voice husky.

"*Huh*, let's," Misshi said softly, wondering if he could see the heat of her cheeks in the moonlight.

He took her hand and led her down onto a soft hill of grass that overlooked the moonlit water of the stream. "I want to know everything about you," Soaring Hawk said.

He slid an arm around her waist and drew her close to him. "You have spoken of a brother. Do you still think of him often?"

"As the years pass, my *tamah-tsi* fades more and more from my memory," Misshi murmured.

She gazed into the softly rippling water, recalling in her mind's eye the freckled face of her older brother, and his laughing green eyes as he playfully wrestled with her as a child.

"But, oh, there are some things I will never forget," she said with a sigh. "I believe I told you before that his name was Dale. Dale Bradley."

"Tell me more."

"We were ever so close as children," Misshi reminisced. "My *tamah-tsi* was older than I. He was my protector. I am sure that when I was taken away by . . . by . . . your renegade father, it devastated my brother. I have worried through the years how he adjusted to my absence. I have worried about him being riddled with guilt that he was not able to protect me."

"I see that it pains you to speak of this part of your past," Soaring Hawk said. "Again I apologize for the wrongs of my father. Had I known then that he had taken you captive, I would have stopped at nothing to save you."

"As you know, I was not his captive for long, so do not despair over it," Misshi said. She turned toward him. She moved to her knees facing him and placed gentle hands on his cheeks. "I was gone from your father's stronghold almost the moment I was taken there. As your father lay on the ground, terribly wounded, no one paid attention to me. It was easy to slip away."

"You were, you still are, a woman of much bravery and heart," Soaring Hawk said. He took her hands from his face, then lowered his mouth to her palms, kissing each.

"I was afraid, oh, so very afraid," Misshi said, a sob escaping as she thought about the terrifying days before she was rescued by Chief Washakie.

"You need never be afraid again," Soaring Hawk said. He reached for her and lifted her so that she was now on his lap. He cradled her close and pressed his nose into the sweet smell of her hair. "My woman, I will always be here to protect you."

"But you will be gone soon to search for your

father," Misshi said. She shivered at the thought of the outcome of that search. She might lose the two men she adored at one blow.

"It will not be for long," Soaring Hawk said, knowing that to be true, for he *did* know the location of the stronghold. It would not take much time to make the attack.

But he still must keep the secret of the location to himself. It wouldn't be long now, though, before he could finally tell his allies.

"Tomorrow, will you go riding with me?" Soaring Hawk asked as Misshi leaned away from him so that their eyes could meet and hold. "It will be a day just for us."

"But . . . it has been so long since I rode a horse," Misshi said. "I am not certain I can remember how."

She blushed at this admission, for Soaring Hawk surely would no longer see her as a strong woman.

"Washakie has never felt it wise for me to travel outside his village," she blurted out. "He did not want the news to spread about my being there."

"Soon everyone will know about you, for no one can stop the news from spreading that I am taking a white wife," Soaring Hawk said. "I will come for you tomorrow. If you knew how to ride a horse when you were younger, the skills will come back quickly. I will teach you how to hone those skills."

"I can't tell you how I have craved such freedom," Misshi said. "Yet still, I feel that—"

"I will take you where no one will see us," Soaring Hawk said, interrupting her. "Trust me, Misshi, as I know Washakie will trust you in my care. I will allow nothing to threaten you."

"Please do come for me, then," Misshi said, her eyes bright with excitement. "I will not sleep this night as I wait for morning to come, and then you."

"Misshi, my sweet Misshi," Soaring Hawk said as he wove his fingers through her thick black hair. "Soon you will be sleeping in my arms every night and awakening in them every morning. After Chief Bear is found and stopped, we can proceed with our marriage plans."

"I wish it were tomorrow," Misshi murmured. She lowered her eyes so that he would not see tears filling them out of fear that what they were planning might not come to pass. If Chief Bear bested Soaring Hawk and Washakie, there would be no marriage. There would be no future for Misshi, for how could she ever love anyone as she loved Soaring Hawk?

Soaring Hawk placed a gentle finger beneath her chin and lifted her face so that he could gaze into her eyes. When he saw a tear stream from one corner, he placed a thumb there and wiped the tear away.

"I do not like to see tears in your eyes," he said thickly. "I know they are from worry about what lies ahead for Soaring Hawk and Washakie. I, too, dread this attack, especially what might happen to my mother during the fight. But whatever happens will be what destiny has planned. Be strong for me, my woman, for I need more strength and courage now than ever before in my life."

"For you, I will be strong," Misshi said, flinging herself into his arms. She clung to him. "I never want to let you down. Never."

"Nor I you," Soaring Hawk said, then again lifted her chin with a finger and lowered his lips to hers to give her an all-consuming kiss. In that kiss was everything they both needed to get them through the coming separation.

Then Misshi drew away from him and smiled. "I doubt that I shall sleep at all tonight," she said excitedly. "Do you truly think I can learn how to ride a horse again? It has been so long."

"You will ride, you will feel the freedom of riding, and you will feel the joy it brings to your heart," Soaring Hawk said, taking her hand and urging her to her feet. "Come now. I shall take you home. Tomorrow is not that far away, nor I. At daybreak I will wait for you at the edge of the village. We shall ride as the birds and animals awaken to another day!"

"How wonderful it sounds," Misshi said, then stopped and stood in his way so that he could not go any farther. She twined her arms around his neck. "But it is still night. Do you think you can kiss me one more time in the moonlight?"

His response was to draw her body next to his.

As nighthawks soared overhead, squawking out their strange night calls and making shadows on the ground around Misshi and Soaring Hawk, they were lost in the wonders of a sweet, deep kiss. The bliss of their embrace caused them both to grow dizzy.

Swaying drunkenly, they laughingly parted, then held hands and ran on toward the village, which was now visible through a break in the trees a short distance away.

Smoke spiraled from the smoke holes of the tepees.

The glow of fires in the lodges could be seen through the buffalo hides.

Somewhere in one of the lodges a mother sang to a child. Elsewhere someone played a flute of love.

"Someone else has discovered love," Soaring Hawk said, smiling down at Misshi. "Do you hear the music of the flute? It is to lure a woman into a man's arms. Since I have already known the feel of your body against mine, a flute serenade is not required unless you wish it."

"You are all I need, not flute music," Misshi murmured, smiling. As they came up behind her tepee, she stopped.

"You'd best not kiss me again, or I will not be able to say good-bye," Misshi confessed, for the kisses tonight had awakened sensual feelings within her that were almost too delicious to deny herself.

She knew that soon they would be free to allow their bodies to come together as they yearned to do. For now, she would cherish her anticipation of that special moment when they did make love.

"I wish I did not have to say good-bye," Soaring Hawk said huskily. "But I must." He turned her toward her tepee. "*Mea,* go. Do not look back, for if I look into your eyes another time tonight, it will be I who will not be able to say good-bye."

Giggling, her hair flying, Misshi ran away from him.

Soaring Hawk watched her, the hunger deep inside him so intense he could hardly stand it.

Sighing heavily, he went to his strawberry roan and mounted it.

He rode hard toward his mountain, his every breath and heartbeat for his Misshi. He was not sure he could deny his yearnings for much longer.

He even wondered if he should put off going horseback riding, for could he deny himself once they were alone?

"I doubt it," he whispered. "I truly doubt it." He had waited so long for the right woman; now that he had found her, he wanted to claim her completely, heart, body, and soul.

Chapter Eleven

I am my beloved's and his desire
is toward me.
   —*Old Testament*
   "The Song of Solomon"

The day had been even more wonderful than Misshi could have imagined. She had ridden out of
the Shoshone village mounted on Soaring Hawk's
strawberry roan, his arm holding her securely
against him. After a while she had tried riding
alone and discovered that her old skills did indeed
come back to her. It was a wonderful discovery.
Ah, how she had loved riding as a child with her
brother. As a woman, she would enjoy it even

more, for she would be with the man she loved.

Afterward, Soaring Hawk had joined her again on his steed, and they had resumed traveling together across the wonders of Wyoming land. She had laughed merrily when the horse startled sleepy, long-eared jackrabbits, amazed at the sudden burst of speed they showed.

They had stopped to rest beside a field of wild strawberries. She had melted inside when he fed her strawberries one by one. She wasn't sure which was the sweeter—the berries or the fingers that fed them to her.

As they rode on, the air was fresh and delightful, sweet with the scent of wildflowers, pine, and cedar. A small red cactus was in bloom; prickly pear grew in profusion as did a nettle which had a lovely white blossom with iridescent, tissue-paper-thin petals, called the Maricopa Lily.

Misshi was fascinated by the prairie-dog towns they were now riding past. She smiled as she watched the little creatures of a dark buckskin-brown color sit erect on the edge of the mounds that surrounded their burrows. They uttered sharp barking sounds and vigorously jerked their short tails against their backs with each scolding bark.

As Soaring Hawk urged his steed onward, Misshi saw several sage hens appear just over a rise of land. They looked like the chickens her mother had kept in a pen for a daily supply of eggs and for their special Sunday dinners of fried chicken, mashed potatoes, milk gravy, and green beans.

While living with the Shoshone she had eaten sage hens and she knew they tasted nothing like those she had eaten as a child. Sage hens tasted like the sage her mother had always used to season her delicious Thanksgiving dressing.

Misshi noticed that Soaring Hawk was directing his horse toward a stream. Wildflowers grew in profusion along the banks. There were pretty blue lupines, and the bright red wild geraniums that the Shoshone used to heal stomach aches. Also she saw lovely purple Canadian violets, and a multitude of sweet-faced daisies.

"Do you see the beauty I promised you?" Soaring Hawk asked as he held Misshi close to him with an arm around her waist, her back to him. "When I wish to be alone with my prayers, I come to this secret place."

He sighed heavily. "One day, though, it will be discovered by whites," he said.

"It is so beautiful," Misshi sighed. "It is as though I am entering a fantasyland."

Frowning, she swatted at a tiny insect that was pestering her. It was a buffalo gnat, which usually annoyed animals instead of humans. She had seen

115

buffalo surrounded by such gnats, their ears and eyes swollen from the many bites.

"I could do without the buffalo gnats," she said, again waving one away from her face. "Otherwise," she went on, "I have never seen such beauty. Should we ride among the flowers? I hate to crush them."

"Where those that are crushed bend low to the earth, others will soon follow in their place," Soaring Hawk told her. "The earth nourishes the roots, so that they multiply and multiply. Even when they are buried beneath winter snows, they survive. In the spring, ah, what a sight to behold as the snow melts away and the plants begin to sprout, with their tiny buds opening so that their faces can catch the flames of the sun."

"I hope to see it," Misshi murmured. "Will you bring me here next spring?"

"Only if you are not heavy with child," Soaring Hawk said. He chuckled when he heard her quick intake of breath at that remark. "You seem taken aback by the idea of a child."

"I have never envisioned myself as a mother. Yet what wonderful joy it brings to my heart to know that we will become parents sometime in the future," Misshi said as he drew rein beside the slowly ambling stream, where flowers hung down like tiny, colorful umbrellas.

"Children," Misshi then said. "I adore the children in my village."

She turned to gaze into Soaring Hawk's eyes as he allowed the reins to go slack in his hand. "Will ours be more in your likeness, do you think, than mine?" she asked softly. "I would love to have a son in your exact image."

"As I will pray for a daughter who is in yours," Soaring Hawk said. He wove a hand through her silkenly soft black hair. "Although you are white, your hair is black like the Shoshone's, so our daughter will no doubt have the same color hair."

He gazed deeply into her eyes, mesmerized anew by their violet color. "What would be truly beautiful would be a daughter whose face is the color of her father's and whose eyes are the color of her mother's," he said. "Would that not be an entrancing combination?"

The mention of her hair being black made Misshi uncomfortable, for she realized that she had not told Soaring Hawk her hair was naturally red.

She started to explain why she had dyed it, but he had slid from the horse and was pulling her into his arms, his lips only a breath away from hers.

"You know what must happen before children are brought into this world, do you not?" Soaring Hawk asked huskily, his dark eyes filled with a sudden longing.

"*Huh*, I know . . ." Misshi said, hoping that he did not see how hard she swallowed at the thought of what he was referring to.

She would never forget how her body had reacted to his kisses and embraces the night before.

She had never felt such blissful longings.

She felt them even now, swelling within her, making a strange warm, delicious sensation within her.

She wanted him so badly she ached. But could she participate in lovemaking? Should she?

In the white world, a young woman was taught not to give herself to a man until vows were spoken. But she reminded herself that she was no longer of that world. She lived in a wild land where life could be cut short at the blink of an eye.

And she *was* going to marry Soaring Hawk.

In the white world, they would be called "engaged" even though she wore no ring to prove it.

Her thoughts were stolen by the wonder of his kiss when he brought his lips down upon hers. He knelt on the flower-covered ground and lowered her to the smiling faces of daisies.

Breathless with desire, Misshi was only scarcely aware of where she was now. Only Soaring Hawk was real to her as his kiss deepened and his hands slowly lifted the skirt of her dress up past her thighs.

He shoved the doeskin garment even higher, and she felt the wind and sun caressing her where no man had touched before. Then one of his hands *was* there, his fingers caressing her. The bliss that accompanied his touch swept away any warning that momentarily flashed inside her consciousness.

When his fingers touched her throbbing mound, and then he slowly rubbed her there, he awoke something within Misshi and made her feel faint with pleasure.

She gasped at how suddenly she was gripped by intense desire.

As one kiss blended into another, an even more delicious languor stole over Misshi. And then Soaring Hawk eased away from her.

She gazed up at him through passion-heavy lashes. Her body turned liquid as his eyes touched that part of her where his fingers had just been, and then she uttered a moan of bliss when he dipped his head low and swept his tongue over her throbbing womanhood.

A blaze of urgency filled her as his tongue continued to pleasure her in a way she would have thought forbidden. But the wild, exuberant passion it created within her made her uncaring of society's rules.

Misshi was lost, heart and soul, to this man.

However he wished to show his love for her, so

be it. She gave herself up to the rapture. She closed her eyes and slowly tossed her head from side to side as the pleasure built inside her.

Then when something within her seemed to explode, to burst into a million pieces of sunshine, warming her through and through with a glorious, sensual release, she gasped and enjoyed it until the pleasurable spasms were over and she was left full of awe.

Her eyes sprang quickly open when she realized that Soaring Hawk no longer caressed her with his tongue.

She found him smiling down at her as she still lay on the cushion of flowers. He was now kneeling between her outstretched legs.

She questioned him with her eyes, for she was still so stunned by what had happened to her body, she could not find the words to question him about it.

She only knew that whatever he had done had awakened a pleasure in her that she would always crave, for even now she wished to experience it again.

"What you have just experienced is the awakening of the true woman in you," Soaring Hawk said huskily. He placed a gentle hand on her cheek. "The pleasure you felt is only a portion of what you will feel when you and I make love together."

"Do you mean that what I just experienced is similar to how it will be when you make love to me?" Misshi murmured, closing her eyes in ecstasy as one of his hands went again to the place where she pleasantly ached, and his fingers began to slowly caress her.

"When we make love, you will know twice the pleasure you just felt and are still feeling," Soaring Hawk said, fighting hard within himself not to fill her with his heat, not to take her all the way to paradise.

His body ached for release. Oh, how he ached to blanket her with his body, hold her close, and fill her with his throbbing need.

Together they would soar high above the clouds in a blazing, searing ecstasy!

But he still felt that he should wait. He wanted to lead her into the bonding of man and woman only after truly preparing her for it.

What he had just done was only the beginning.

It was so hard, though, with his manhood throbbing unmercifully, not to make love with her. But he knew the art of restraint and he would now practice it.

"I must take you home now," he said, understanding the surprise in her eyes at that sudden announcement.

"Truly? You must?" Misshi asked, watching him move away from her.

She wanted to grab his hand and place it back where her body throbbed with desire. She wanted to beg for more.

Yet she knew that was wrong and fought to take more control of her desires. She shoved the skirt of her dress down, covering herself.

"I am certain that Washakie will not rest until you are safely home again," Soaring Hawk said, rising to his feet. He reached a hand out for her. "Come. I do not want to worry my friend Washakie, nor do you."

When she took his hand, she realized it was trembling, and wondered if it was because he had not received sexual pleasure himself today as she had.

She felt as though she might be cheating him by leaving it that way until their next sexual encounter, yet she was unskilled at sexual play and would not know where to begin unless he taught her.

That would come later.

She understood the importance of returning to the Shoshone village. But she would live to be with Soaring Hawk again.

"*Ka*, no, I do not wish to worry Washakie," Mis-shi murmured, but as she started to walk to Soaring Hawk's horse, he reached out and circled her waist, drawing her against him.

"*Nei-com-man-pe-ein*, I love you, woman," Soaring Hawk said huskily, then crushed her lips with a heated kiss and ground his body into hers until they both moaned.

Breathing hard, still feeling it best to delay what his body was crying out for, Soaring Hawk swept Misshi fully into his arms and carried her to his strawberry roan and placed her in the Indian saddle.

After mounting behind her, he wheeled his horse around and rode back in the direction of the Shoshone village.

Their route took them through deep canyons, up and down the vast hilly terrain, and across wide-open spaces of blowing grass.

Then they entered the darkness of a forest. Soaring Hawk slowly wove his way through it. And once again they were traveling across a flat, open stretch of land that was the only place where they might be spotted together.

Misshi scarcely breathed as she watched for any sign of movement. Suddenly she grabbed Soaring Hawk's arm and squeezed. Up ahead along the trail she saw a sight that brought back memories so vivid, she was a young girl again crouched low behind a wagon as her father tried to protect her from attacking Indians. She squeezed her eyes closed as she relived the moment the arrow slammed into her father's chest.

She was not even aware of sobbing until Soaring Hawk reached out and drew her face down against his chest in an effort to protect her from seeing what she knew was an Indian slaughter. She had already seen the overturned wagons still smoldering, sending spirals of smoke into the beautiful blue sky. Vultures were circling overhead, their beady eyes searching out their next meal among the bodies that lay strewn here and there over the blood-spattered land.

Soaring Hawk drew rein and stopped his horse, for he now also saw something else. There was a large buffalo kill not far from the scene of the human slaughter.

His eyebrows lifted. Like the whites, the buffalo seemed to have been the victims of someone with a crazed mind.

He was swept by a feeling of horror as he realized that whoever was committing this mindless mayhem was doing it more frequently than before.

"Soaring Hawk, how could this have happened?" Misshi cried, still not looking. "And do you think . . .

anyone . . . survived? Could they be hiding? Or could they have run off?"

"By the looks of things, I do not believe there are survivors," Soaring Hawk said.

He gazed from body to body and saw the arrows protruding from them; flies buzzed over bloody heads where scalps had been removed.

"Please go and see?" Misshi said softly, unwilling to go any closer to the massacre herself.

"I cannot leave you alone while I look," Soaring Hawk said. He placed a finger beneath her chin and lifted it so that their eyes could meet. "Those responsible for this kill might be close enough to grab you while I am away."

"Then go and I will go with you; I shall keep my eyes closed," Misshi gulped out.

Soaring Hawk nodded, brushed a kiss across her brow, then moved his horse forward at a slow lope.

When he reached the wagons, he rode from body to body until all were examined. As he had thought, there were no survivors.

Then he rode closer to the dead buffalo.

He grew cold inside as he discovered that this buffalo kill was not made by Indians, as those who had killed today must wish it to seem.

The hunters had used arrows as Indians would, but Soaring Hawk could tell from a buffalo head whether or not it was an Indian kill. If there was a hole in the forehead, the animal was slaughtered by an Indian. It was through this opening that he extracted the brains, which were always removed for use in the treatment of skins.

These buffalo were not killed in such a manner, nor were brains extracted from the buffalo. In fact, no part of the buffalo had been taken. They certainly had not been killed for their meat or skins.

With Misshi still hiding her eyes against his powerful chest, he rode back to the scene of the human slaughter.

He looked more closely at the victims now and saw signs that made him doubt that Indians were the attackers. He was almost certain that this was the work of white people trying to make it look like an Indian ambush.

His thoughts went suddenly to his renegade father, and all of the attacks that he was being blamed for. Might some of those have been done by whites trying to stir up trouble for the red man in this area?

The possibility that his father was not responsible for the savagery of the recent kills made him hope that his father was not the fiend he was made out to be.

Soaring Hawk vowed that he would find those who were to blame!

If he could believe that his father's life had changed, and that he now walked the path of peace, Soaring Hawk would reconsider his plans to go after his father.

Should he and Washakie be looking for someone else?

But who?

Who could hate Indians so much that he would go to such lengths to make the red man look fiendish?

"Soaring Hawk, you are quiet," Misshi said as he rode away from the kill.

"I have much to think about," Soaring Hawk mumbled. "I have much to talk over with Washakie."

She saw pain etched across his handsome face and thought she knew what had caused it. If his father had done this terrible deed, it must hurt Soaring Hawk terribly to know that he was blood kin to such a villain.

She said no more, for she felt he needed time to think before reaching Washakie's village. Once they arrived, he would need to discuss it all with his trusted confidant.

She still sat facing him, her legs straddling him as she laid her cheek against his chest. She could hear the pounding of his heart and hear the short intakes of his breath. Was he seeing all over again the scene of the slaughter?

They rode onward in silence that was broken only when they reached Washakie's village.

Misshi sat in Washakie's lodge with Soaring Hawk as Soaring Hawk solemnly related what they had come across and why he felt this was the work of white men.

Soon after, Misshi stood outside her lodge and watched as Washakie, Soaring Hawk, and several of Washakie's warriors left for Fort Bridger to tell Colonel Harry Braddock about the newest slaughter.

Misshi knew that Soaring Hawk was also going to ask if Colonel Braddock knew any whites in the area who might have a reason to make this attack look like the work of Indians. Someone like that could cause a war between the red and white peoples.

Misshi shivered at that thought, for she knew that if such warring began, it might mean the end of the Shoshone. They could not hope to stand against the cavalry.

Misshi ran inside her tepee and sat down before the lodge fire, but not even the warmth of the flames could take away the chill that had engulfed her at that grim vision of the future.

She hid her face in her hands and sobbed when

she thought of Soaring Hawk and the dreams they had for their future.

Those, too, could be dashed under the spattering of gunfire and arrows!

Chapter Twelve

Love is enough, tho the world be awaning.
—William Morris
"Love Is Enough" (1872)

Soaring Hawk and Washakie sat uncomfortably in stiff-backed chairs in Colonel Braddock's office at Fort Bridger as Washakie explained their reason for coming.

As the golden-haired colonel sat behind his desk, attired in fringed buckskins instead of his usual blue uniform, he gazed intently at Washakie.

Soaring Hawk studied the colonel, sizing him up. It was necessary to be friends with this white cavalryman.

131

For the most part, the Shoshone and the Bannock tribes were hospitable to traders and the military. Forts meant goods for their people, and although goods might promote dependency, they also lessened hardships.

Before the building of forts in this area, packaged goods and industrial items could be obtained only by long and dangerous trips to the Mandan villages on the upper Missouri River, or to the Comanche in Nebraska and Kansas.

Yet for all the desirability of their goods, the white men lived in a strange fashion. Soaring Hawk's eyes strayed around the room, noting its oddities.

The lodge, where this colonel not only worked but also lived, was crudely made of logs, as were the tables and chairs that were positioned in what he saw as illogical places. His attention was drawn to the pot-bellied stove at the far side of the room. He knew that during the coldest months of winter this strange apparatus would glow orange from the fire burning within.

It was nothing at all like Soaring Hawk's warm lodge fire, where the fire was free to warm the flesh.

And then there was the door that led to the living quarters. It was closed, but he could smell the aroma of food cooking and he could hear the soft laughter of a child.

He was fascinated by the creature that was hidden behind the closed door. The four-year-old girl had called it a cat. She had offered her pet to Soaring Hawk to hold, but he had hesitated, for the only cats he was familiar with were the wildcats that roamed the land.

But when he finally held the cat and the child instructed him to stroke its sleek black fur, the cat emitted a soft sort of purring sound. Soaring Hawk's eyes had lit up with pleasure.

"And, Soaring Hawk, you too feel that this recent atrocity was performed by white people, not Indians?" Colonel Braddock asked, drawing Soaring Hawk's eyes back to him.

"*Huh*, it *was* suspicious," Soaring Hawk said. He gazed at the colonel across the large oak desk piled high with journals and a scattering of papers. The wick of a kerosene lamp on the desk gave off soft light and what Soaring Hawk thought was a strange odor.

"The more I think about it, the more I believe that it was all done by whites to make it *look* like the vicious acts of Indians," Soaring Hawk said.

Soaring Hawk leaned forward in the chair. His gaze locked with the colonel's. He tried not to be unnerved when the colonel idly toyed with a tiny wooden sculpture of a bear.

"Do you know of the arrival of new white people

in this area who might be responsible for these atrocities?" Soaring Hawk asked.

Colonel Braddock frowned.

He placed the bear sculpture on the desk, then leaned back in his chair and folded his arms across his narrow chest.

"The only new arrivals are cavalrymen at a new fort that has been built downriver . . . Fort Adams," he said.

"I am not aware of a new fort," Washakie said, his dark eyes narrowing.

"Nor I," Soaring Hawk said, his eyes still on the colonel.

"It has only recently been established, but don't even think about holding them responsible for such atrocious acts," Colonel Braddock quickly said. "These soldiers are carefully chosen men. They are here to keep peace, not stir up trouble that would begin a war."

When neither Soaring Hawk nor Washakie commented, Colonel Braddock cleared his throat nervously and slowly unfolded his arms.

"I think it would be wise to suggest that those at Fort Adams join me and my cavalrymen, and you, Chief Washakie and Chief Soaring Hawk, to search for the murderers," Colonel Braddock said, his jaw tight. "What do you think of that suggestion? Surely with your knowledge of the land, and with our gun power, we can a track down the damn varmints like a coon hound sniffs out coons."

Not familiar at all with what a "coon hound" might be, much less a "coon," Soaring Hawk ignored the reference. He nodded. "Yes, I agree to the plan," he said, then glanced at Washakie. "And how do you feel? Would your warriors join forces willingly with the cavalrymen?"

"If that will bring justice to those who are doing the killing, yes, I will join forces with the soldiers," Washakie said. "It has been many moons since I rode on any expedition, but I will do so again if it is for the betterment of our people."

Soaring Hawk smiled, nodded, then gazed at Colonel Braddock again. "Tell us more about the new fort and give us the name of the man in charge," he said, eager to get on with their plans.

"The colonel who came with the men to build the new fort died shortly after their arrival," Colonel Braddock said. "Word was sent to Washington about his death. Another colonel will arrive in the near future to take his place. The fort was completed under another man's command, and the soldiers are under his command until the new colonel arrives."

He rose from his chair and went to gaze out a window. "The man in charge was deemed the most reliable of those who came with Colonel Adams," he said, then turned and faced Soaring Hawk and Washakie, clasping his hands together behind him. "The man in charge is Major Dale Bradley. He is an eager young man who will work his way quickly up through the ranks." He smiled. "As ambitious as he is, I see him one day becoming an even more powerful colonel than myself."

The name Dale Bradley leaped out at Soaring Hawk and Washakie at once. They looked quickly at each other.

Washakie had known that name for years, for Misshi had said it often during her conversation about the brother she doubted she would ever see again. Soaring Hawk had heard her speak it just that morning.

This Major Dale Bradley, who was in charge at Fort Adams, was Misshi's brother. In silence, they communicated with one another with their eyes, both understanding that it was best not to tell Colonel Braddock of this discovery.

It was something they both felt was best left unsaid until they could see the sort of man Major Bradley was. Had he arrived in Wyoming with vengeance heavy on his heart . . . vengeance for a sister who had been taken from him by redskins?

"You both have gone quiet," Colonel Braddock said, stepping closer to Soaring Hawk and Washakie. "What was it that I said?"

Soaring Hawk and Washakie stood up, facing Colonel Braddock.

"We would like to go now to Fort Adams and talk with this Major Bradley," Soaring Hawk said, ignoring the colonel's puzzlement. "Already we have waited one sunrise too long to come to you about the atrocities in the area. There was another act of violence while we foolishly waited to come to Fort Bridger to speak with you. Let us not delay any longer."

Washakie nodded. "Yes, it is best that we proceed today to Fort Adams," he said. "We will have council with the man in charge."

"I will accompany you to Fort Adams," Colonel Braddock said. He grabbed a rifle, then went and opened the door to the outside.

The journey to Fort Adams was a silent one. All three men were on the lookout for possible ambushes.

When they reached Fort Adams, with its tall palisaded fence, Colonel Braddock saluted the two guards that stood just outside the opened gates, then rode inside with Washakie and Soaring Hawk and dismounted before the main cabin in the center of the courtyard.

Just as they started to step up on the cabin's porch, the door opened with a jerk, halting them in mid-stride.

Soaring Hawk was taken aback by the resemblance between this man and Misshi. Except for the color of their hair and eyes, they had strikingly similar features. Soaring Hawk was convinced that Dale Bradley was indeed Misshi's brother.

But there was one other notable difference between Misshi and Dale Bradley. In the depths of this man's green eyes was nothing but coldness. As Major Bradley stared at them, Soaring Hawk began to believe there was also loathing in his look.

"Come inside," Dale said icily after Colonel Braddock introduced them.

Soaring Hawk grew cold when he saw how Dale hurriedly wiped his hand on his buckskin breeches after shaking both Washakie and Soaring Hawk's hands, as though wiping away filth that he had gotten from touching a red man.

They went inside and were seated before Dale's oak desk, while he sat behind it on a leather chair. Soaring Hawk glanced at Colonel Braddock to see if he had noticed Major Bradley's openly displayed prejudice.

Soaring Hawk was disappointed when he saw nothing to indicate that Colonel Braddock realized this major was not suited for the job he had been sent to do. Or perhaps Colonel Braddock had seen it and did not care.

Suddenly Soaring Hawk felt afraid that both he

and Washakie had misjudged Colonel Braddock. Kind and peace-loving, Washakie had perhaps not *wanted* to see the bad side of Colonel Braddock. If Colonel Braddock did not care that a man like Dale Bradley was in charge of a full unit of cavalrymen at Fort Adams, then Major Braddock truly did not care about the fate of the Indians in the territory. Soaring Hawk feared that their situation was worse than he had initially thought.

To have two forts governed by the wrong kind of man might mean disaster for the Shoshone and Bannock peoples.

Soaring Hawk thought of Misshi and how much he wanted to protect her. Would he be able to now?

Were these two white men in charge of these forts possibly even plotting together against his people? That thought gave Soaring Hawk an uneasy feeling in the pit of his stomach.

"Major Bradley, I'm sure you've heard of Chief Washakie, a man of peace, but I doubt that you have heard of Chief Soaring Hawk," Colonel Braddock said. "He too is a man of peace, yet he is too young to have made his mark yet as Washakie has done."

Colonel Braddock smiled across the desk at Dale, who had yet to say much about anything. Dale's green eyes were guarded as he shifted them back and forth between Washakie and Soaring Hawk.

"Major Bradley, Chief Soaring Hawk is from the Bannock tribe, kin to the Shoshone," Colonel Braddock explained.

At those words Dale gave an audible gasp. He rose from his chair and went to stand directly over Soaring Hawk. In his eyes was visible hatred as he stared down at the Bannock chief.

Refusing to be intimidated, Soaring Hawk stood up and smiled when Major Bradley, who was not as tall as he, was forced to look up at him.

"Do you have something to say to Soaring Hawk?" Soaring Hawk asked, his voice as tight as the string on his bow. "Or is it all being said in your eyes?"

"What the hell's going on here?" Colonel Braddock demanded, rushing from his chair as Washakie also rose and stood stiffly beside Soaring Hawk. "What's between you two that I don't know? Do you two know one another, or what?" he asked, raising an eyebrow. "I've never seen such coldness between two people. If looks could kill, you'd both be dead by now."

"This man is from the very tribe that took my sister captive," Major Bradley finally said, his voice a dark, low hiss. "Where is she, Soaring Hawk? Surely you know Chief Bear. He's the one who took my sister. Tell me, Soaring Hawk. Do you know Chief Bear? Do you know of my sister's whereabouts?" He swallowed hard. "Do you know if she's even alive?"

"Hey, now, let's just slow down here," Colonel Braddock said as he saw the look of hate being exchanged between the two men. Fearing a fight, he interposed himself between Major Bradley and Soaring Hawk. He grabbed Dale by the arm and led him back around behind his desk and shoved him down into his chair. "We can talk about this peacefully, now can't we?"

"All right," Dale grumbled. "I'm just not used to coming face to face with a member of the tribe that stole my sister."

"But you forget that the man who abducted her is not really part of the Bannocks," Colonel Braddock said. He placed his fists on his hips. "Major Bradley, Chief Bear broke away from the tribe. He is a leader of renegades. *This* Bannock chief, Chief Soaring Hawk, is a man of peace. He had come with Washakie to hunt down those who are responsible for the recent slaughters."

He turned and faced Soaring Hawk. "And even though Chief Bear is his father, Soaring Hawk is willing to do everything possible to stop him," he said.

"Father?" Dale screeched out as he flew from his

141

chair. "Are you saying that this Indian is the son of Chief Bear?"

"He is, by blood ties, my father, but where it matters, in the heart, I no longer claim him as kin," Soaring Hawk said quietly. "His way is not my way. Long ago my mother taught me to be different from my father. When I reached an age when I could take charge of my own destiny, I left my father's home. I made my own home with my own warriors. I strive for peace and justice. I have sworn to hunt down and stop my father, no matter how it must be done. The important thing is that we should work together now for the same cause, even though you obviously hate all men whose skin is red. It shows in your voice. I see it in your eyes. So do not try to claim friendship, when it is not there."

Breathing hard, his eyes spitting fire, Major Bradley brushed past Colonel Braddock and glared up at Soaring Hawk. "Surely you were there when your father brought my sister to his stronghold," he hissed out. "Surely you can tell me what her fate was."

Fear claimed Soaring Hawk's heart, for the last thing on earth that he wanted to do was to tell this prejudiced man anything about his sister Misshi.

A man of such prejudice would no longer see his

sister as white. He would see her as more Indian than white because she had lived among the Shoshone for so long.

Soaring Hawk had heard tales of captured white women who had lived for many years with Indians. Sometimes when they were rescued by whites, they were killed because their own people believed them soiled.

He could never allow that to happen to Misshi.

"No, I was not there when my father brought home a white woman captive," Soaring Hawk said blandly. He was not lying. Misshi had been brought to his father's stronghold just after Soaring Hawk had fled to live his own life.

"And once I left my father's home, I never returned," Soaring Hawk quickly added. "What he does, he does without my blessing."

Soaring Hawk heard Washakie inhale a soft breath of relief. Misshi's presence among his people was still a secret.

"All right, big man, that has to do, for I can't drag words from inside you," Dale hissed out. "But we shall see just how truthful you are being when we find your father's stronghold. We shall see just how much you hate your renegade father. You will be given the first shot at him."

Dale sighed heavily, then said, "If we do not find Misshi there, we must see if there is a reddish gold scalp on the old renegade's scalp pole. If so, it is proof he killed my Misshi, for her hair was the same color as mine."

Soaring Hawk was startled. He had never seen Misshi with that color hair; he had never guessed that black was not the true color of her hair. He had to refrain from looking at Washakie, for that might awaken Dale's suspicions.

Instead, Soaring Hawk held his eyes steady on Major Bradley. "We have not come here today to speak only of hunting down my father," he said. "We have come to make plans to find those who are responsible for the latest atrocities in the area."

A slow, mocking smile fluttered across Soaring Hawk's lips. "You see, I do not believe that Chief Bear is responsible for the recent killings," he said, watching the major's reaction to what he was saying. "The kills have been too sloppy. I see this as the work of whites trying to look like Indians."

When Soaring Hawk saw Major Bradley turn pale, he knew that he had hit a nerve.

Excitement filled him to think that perhaps he had already found the culprit he was looking for. Yet it was sad that it was Misshi's brother. When she knew the truth, if it was true, it would devastate her, for she had only sweet memories of her brother.

Soaring Hawk hated to be the one to interfere

with such memories, yet Misshi had to know the truth, good or bad.

"Do you think you might know any whites in the area who hate my people so much that they would kill unmercifully to make it look like Indians' work?" Soaring Hawk asked, unable to keep a taunting note from his voice.

He enjoyed seeing the white man squirm as he shuffled his feet nervously and clasped his hands tightly behind him.

It was hard for Soaring Hawk to understand how this man could be so bad and Misshi so good, yet was it not the same in his own family? His father was evil through and through, and Soaring Hawk wanted nothing but peace and goodness.

"No, I know of no white people who might do such a thing as that," Dale said, his lisp growing worse as he became more tense. "But I will keep a watch out for such culprits."

"You do that," Soaring Hawk said, his voice smooth and again taunting.

"I think enough has been said for one day," Colonel Braddock said. "I think it's best that we leave."

Although no set plans had been made for an alliance with the white men, Soaring Hawk was eager to be away from this fort and the man who was in charge. He had come close to openly accusing Major Dale Bradley of committing the atrocities. He knew that it was best to avoid any accusations until he had absolute proof.

After getting outside the gates, Colonel Braddock went one way on his steed, Washakie and Soaring Hawk, another.

As the two chiefs rode back toward the Shoshone village, they were at first silent. Then, as though they knew each other's minds, they both stopped, wheeled their horses around, and stared at the fort which was now some distance from them.

"This man who is Misshi's brother is hiding something," Soaring Hawk blurted out. "He has evil in his eyes. I truly believe that our hunt for the killer stops at Fort Adams. Dale Bradley is the sort who could kill so heartlessly."

"We must not tell Misshi that her brother is in the area," Washakie said. "Nor should we mention our suspicions about him, for I feel the same as you about him."

"I usually agree with everything you say, but this time, Washakie, I have a different opinion," Soaring Hawk said softly, and with much respect. "Although we both have bad feelings about doing it, I truly believe Misshi should know, that she should be told her brother is in Wyoming land, and close to your village. It will be more painful to hear it from someone else and know that we kept the truth from her."

Washakie thought hard for a moment as he continued staring at the fort, then turned slowly to Soaring Hawk. "*Huh*, you are right," he said thickly. "You will soon marry Misshi. It is best not to enter into a marriage with secrets held from the woman who will be your wife. And it is only fair that she should know about her brother."

Soaring Hawk nodded. "And she should be told everything about him, not only the part that is good, that he is alive," Soaring Hawk said.

Washakie nodded. "*Huh*, we will tell her even the worst," he said softly. "We will tell her our suspicions about what we think her brother is responsible for."

They went on their way, their hearts heavy with what must be done.

Chapter Thirteen

As sweet and musical
As bright Apollo's lute, strung with his hair;
And when love speaks, the voice of all the gods
Makes heaven drowsy with the harmony.
— Shakespeare
"Love's Labour's Lost" Act IV

The fire had burned to low embers in the firepit in Washakie's tepee. Washakie was seated on his plush pelts beside the fire as Soaring Hawk sat with Misshi on the other side of the fire from him. Soaring Hawk was the one speaking as Washakie sat listening and watching for her reaction.

149

Soaring Hawk could feel Misshi's hands begin to tremble.

As Misshi listened, she was so stunned, she could only stare at Soaring Hawk. When he was through telling her everything about her brother, she was at a loss for words. That her brother might be capable of the recent atrocities was incomprehensible to her. Surely Soaring Hawk was wrong.

Yet Washakie, wise man that he was, seemed as convinced as Soaring Hawk that Dale could have done those things.

She didn't know how to feel. She was elated to know that her brother was alive and well. But she was sad that her brother had been proven a man of prejudice. Even if he was not the one terrorizing the community, her brother had treated Soaring Hawk and Washakie with coldness and disrespect.

His changed personality was surely a result of her abduction, she thought, shivering at the thought of coming face to face with Dale. Would he treat *her* the same as he had treated Soaring Hawk and Washakie?

Soaring Hawk saw the pain in Misshi's eyes. He wrapped her in his arms and held her close.

"You will get past your pain and shock over how your brother has changed," Soaring Hawk said, slowly caressing her back with his hand. "I will make it so. So will Washakie. And your brother

does not know you are living with the Shoshone.
He does not even have to know that you are alive.
I think it would be best if you forget that he is
near. Think, instead, of our upcoming marriage
and the children we are going to bring into the
world."

"That sounds so wonderful," Misshi murmured.
She eased herself from Soaring Hawk's arms, wiped
a tear from her cheek, then gazed at him. "But that
would be too easy. I have never run away from
anything. Nor shall I now. I must go and see my
brother. Because of what we once were to each
other, I must let him know that I am alive. It has
surely been torment for him not to know my fate."

She turned her eyes to Washakie. "But what will
he see when he looks at me?" she asked. "I am
Shoshone now, heart and soul, and I am not sure
if I could bear to see my brother look at me with
the same prejudice he has shown you."

She reached up and ran her fingers through her
long black hair. Soaring Hawk watched her, only
now remembering what her brother had said about
Misshi's hair being the color of a setting sun. He
raised an eyebrow as he tried to envision her with
hair the color of flame, enhancing her lovely pink
skin. She would be even more beautiful, he
thought.

"My hair," Misshi murmured. "I purposely

changed the color so that I could blend in better with my Shoshone brothers and sisters. When my brother sees *that* choice I have made, it might be the last straw. He may wish to thrust a knife into my heart the moment he sees me.

"Still, I have no choice but to go and meet with my brother," she said. "It is the only human thing to do. It would not be right to let him go on wondering about my fate."

The part of her that had idolized her big brother was again remembering that time so long ago when they had loved each other so dearly. She remembered the sound of his voice as he spoke her name.

She ached to have one of his bear hugs.

She ached to hear his laughter as she had when they'd playfully wrestled in the fresh new grasses of spring.

She recalled how he had taught her to place a worm on one of the fish hooks that he was so skilled at making. She had caught a good-sized largemouth bass at the end of her fishing line, one that had outweighed those her brother had caught that day. To retaliate, Dale had dropped a fat worm down the front of her blouse.

"Misshi?"

Soaring Hawk's voice brought Misshi back to the present.

"I was thinking of some wonderful times with

my brother before our world was turned upside down as we traveled west on the wagon train," Misshi said, sniffling as she wiped more tears from her face. "I do have some wonderful, sweet memories of my brother. I must make sure I do not lose them if I discover he is now very different. It is the good times that I will always remember. Not the bad."

Washakie rose to his feet. He went to Misshi and Soaring Hawk and drew them close, placing an arm around each of them.

He looked from one to the other, ending with his gaze on Misshi. "And it is your final decision that you should go to Fort Adams and see your brother?" he asked.

Misshi nodded. "*Huh*, that is my final decision," she confirmed. "If I didn't, I would always wonder how it might have been to come face to face with my brother again."

Swallowing hard, she stepped away from Washakie. "I would like to go to Fort Adams now, please," she said, her eyes pleading with Washakie, and then Soaring Hawk.

"Then, daughter, I give you my blessing, and, Soaring Hawk, I think it is best for you to take her. I urge you not to travel alone with Misshi to Fort Adams," he said. "Take several of my warriors

153

with you. It will take too long for you to return to your stronghold to get yours."

"Please do not insist on warriors traveling with us," Misshi said. "Soaring Hawk is capable of escorting me to Fort Adams. And . . . and . . . I prefer not to be with anyone now *except* Soaring Hawk. I have so much to adjust to. Being with him, alone, is best for me."

"When you arrive at Fort Adams, who can say what your brother will do?" Washakie said, his voice drawn. "You might need several warriors to make certain you get out of that fort, and safely home again."

"My brother, although changed, will surely be glad to see me and know that I am alive. Surely he will not actually harm me . . . not even when he sees that I am more Shoshone than white."

Washakie and Soaring Hawk exchanged troubled glances; then Soaring Hawk reached a hand over and rested it on Washakie's shoulder. "I promise not to allow anything to happen to Misshi," he said. "She will be safe with me."

Washakie took a deep breath, then gave a quiet nod of acceptance. "Yes, I know that she will be safe with you," he said softly. "Go. My prayers will travel with you."

"Washakie, after Misshi has her meeting with her brother, I would like to have your permission to take her to my home," Soaring Hawk said. "I would like her to see my stronghold and village. I would like to acquaint her with my people and let them meet her, the woman who will soon be their chief's wife and their Bannock princess. I would like to ask your permission for Misshi to spend the night with me and my people."

Washakie gave Misshi a questioning gaze. When he saw that she was eager to go, he nodded, then gave them one last hug before they left for Fort Adams.

After getting permission from Washakie to take one of his horses for her journey to Fort Adams, Misshi went to his corral and chose a gentle mare.

Soon she and Soaring Hawk were on their way to Fort Adams.

As they rode, Soaring Hawk glanced from time to time at Misshi's hair. In the sun he could see traces of red through the black.

"It was a surprise to learn that your true hair color is not as it appears now," Soaring Hawk said, drawing her eyes around to him.

"I will let it grow out to its true color if that is what you wish of me," she murmured.

Soaring Hawk smiled. "Although you do look more Shoshone with the hair color of your adopted people, I would like to at least once see the hair color you were born with," he said.

"After I know that I am with child, *our* child, I will not color my hair again until our child is born," she said, pleased to see how her words made his eyes light up. "My wonderful Bannock chief, don't you know that I would do anything for you? I would even cut every inch of my hair from my head if that is what you desire of me."

Soaring Hawk threw his head back in a fit of laughter. "My woman, I would love you however you are," he said.

Misshi's mood changed rapidly, and Soaring Hawk saw tears fill her eyes even as their shared laughter faded away.

"Talk of hair has not taken my mind off my brother," she said, her voice breaking. "Soaring Hawk, I . . . I . . . am not sure if I can go through with this today, after all. My *tah-mah* won't know me. My hair is different and so am I. I am much older. And . . . and . . . I am dressed like an Indian. I have the feelings of an Indian. Will Dale even believe me when I tell him I am his sister Misshi?"

She swallowed hard. "Soaring Hawk, I want more time to think about this," she said softly. "I can't go to the fort. Not yet."

"Do you mean to say you wish to return to your village?" Soaring Hawk asked.

"*Huh.* I just cannot see myself facing my *tah-mah* quite yet," Misshi murmured. "Is that all right? Do you mind returning me to my home?" Then her eyes lit up. "No, not *my* home. *Yours.* You said you wanted me to know your people and to see your stronghold. Take me there, Soaring Hawk, instead of to the fort, or my own village."

Soaring Hawk looked to his left, in the direction of his stronghold, then stopped his horse. "We are too far from my stronghold to arrive there before night falls," he said. "I do not want to risk traveling those dangerous mountain paths with you during the dusk hours. Instead, we will make camp, then travel to my stronghold early tomorrow morning."

"*Huh*, tomorrow," Misshi said, nodding. She thought ahead to the night, when they would sit beside a campfire beneath the moon and stars.

It gave her a sensual shiver to think what might happen tonight.

"Come," Soaring Hawk said, nodding at Misshi. "Let us find a safe place to make camp."

He knew that this night would not pass without their coming together as lovers!

Chapter Fourteen

Paradise itself were dim
And joyless if not shared with him!
                    —Thomas Moore

Misshi and Soaring Hawk had bathed in a gentle stream while the sun was still there to kiss and warm the water.

They now lay on a blanket beside a cozy campfire beneath the vault of heaven that nightly spread its myriad of bright stars over Wyoming land. The moon was full tonight, bathing everything in a white sheen.

Soaring Hawk lowered himself over Misshi,

trembling with anticipation as their naked bodies touched.

His fingers were twined with Misshi's as she held her arms above her head. Her eyes closed as his kiss deepened.

Forgetting the strange night sounds all around her, sounds made by restless birds in the cotton-wood and box elder trees along the stream, and wolves from somewhere in the distant hills, Misshi realized that she would soon know the true meaning of being a woman. Ah, she could feel the heat of Soaring Hawk's manhood as it lightly probed where she ached to have him enter.

When he gently nudged her legs farther apart with his knee, giving him better access to her, she sighed and moaned, and he shoved further into the folds of her womanhood.

She would never forget the moment when she had first seen him fully unclothed. She had already known the magnificence of his muscled body, but seeing him totally naked had proven just how generous *Wakonda* had been to him. He was very well endowed, and she had wondered if he might even be too large to enter her body.

He had seen her wondering look, and perhaps even the slight fear in her eyes. He'd explained to her that she had nothing to fear. Once he was inside her, she would know just how right they were for each other.

He had warned, though, that for a brief moment there would be pain, but had explained further that that was how it was for all women the first time they made love.

And then, he had said between kisses, that brief pain would turn into pleasure so intense it would be almost magical.

She had recalled the pleasure she had received earlier, when he had made love to her with his lips, tongue, and hands, and knew that she would accept any pain that was necessary to reach that bliss again. And he had told her that she would feel even more pleasure than she had when he had introduced her body to such feelings.

So now, she was breathless as he shoved even further into her.

She felt his fingers tighten around hers when she groaned out the pain that she was experiencing as he pushed past the barrier that proved no man had been there before him.

And then, as he had said, it was all rainbows and sugar candy. The feelings he aroused in her were almost unbearably beautiful and sweet.

Once she had surrendered her all to him, Soaring Hawk moved his lips to the hollow of her throat and kissed her there. His movements within her became rhythmic and deep, each thrust sending a new message of love to her heart.

His lips went to a breast, and he sucked a nipple between his teeth and nibbled on it while thrusting even deeper within her. She could feel a golden web of magic spinning around them as exquisite sensations spiraled through her body.

He then placed his lips next to her ear and reverently breathed her name.

She separated her fingers from his and brought her hands down to twine her arms around his neck.

"Soaring Hawk, my Soaring Hawk," she whispered to him. Her breath quickened when his lips crushed hers beneath a kiss all-consuming, his hands now on her breasts, kneading.

Her body moved rhythmically with his, their groans of pleasure filling the night air, even challenging the cries of the nighthawks as they swept down from the sky to catch the insects drawn toward the flames of the campfire.

Soaring Hawk felt the red hot embers of desire spreading within him as the curl of heat grew in his loins, fueling the passion that had lain smoldering just under the surface until now.

His tongue lapped at her nipple, and he smiled when he heard her moans of pleasure. His hands swept down across her body, causing shivers of excitement wherever he touched.

Again he brought his lips to her mouth and kissed her. He surrounded her with his hard, strong arms, and fiercely held her to him. His mouth forced her lips apart as his kiss grew more and more passionate.

Misshi felt the urgency building. She was almost frantic with this passion that was so new to her.

She moaned in ecstasy when she felt the pleasure building, building, spreading, and then as his body spasmed into hers, she cried out in sweet agony and gave herself over to the wild ecstasy that filled her very being.

Their bodies were quiet now, yet Soaring Hawk still lay over Misshi. His hands moved over the smooth skin of her breasts, his lips following with soft, sensual kisses.

Misshi closed her eyes and enjoyed these precious moments.

Then when Soaring Hawk finally slid away from her and stretched out on his back on the blankets, his eyes smiled into hers. She turned on her side and faced him.

She wished that tonight would never end. She had found paradise with this man and hated to think of the many ways she might lose him.

She forced such thoughts from her mind and kissed him gently on the lips.

163

"You found pleasure?" Soaring Hawk asked, turning to face her.

He slowly ran a hand up and down her hip, fighting off the need to touch her again where he had just filled her with his heat, and then his seed. He would never get enough of this woman.

He was glad that he had waited for her instead of marrying someone else just for the convenience of having a woman to warm his blankets at night.

"I never knew such pleasure could exist, 'til now," Misshi murmured. "And I never knew that I could find a man I would love as I love you."

"Destiny brought us together," Soaring Hawk said, "Our combined destinies."

Suddenly there were several nighthawks sweeping down through the smoke of the campfire. Frightened, Misshi bolted to a sitting position and drew a blanket up around her.

"Why are they here?" she asked, watching the flight of the birds. "Soaring Hawk, why are there so many?"

Soaring Hawk brought a blanket around his shoulders as he scooted over next to Misshi. He, too, watched the soaring, circling, dipping hawks.

"They are not interested in us," he said, chuckling. "They are not even aware of us sitting here watching them. Their only thought is how much food they can get inside their stomachs before the opportunity passes them by."

"I do see how first one and then another captures a bug in its beak, then flies off with it," Misshi said, still watching them.

"The fire's glow and the brightness of the moon have kept them in the sky longer than usual tonight," Soaring Hawk softly explained. "It is at dusk they get their fill of bugs, for it is at dusk that many insects leave their hiding places in the grass and, like lightning bugs, seek their place in the air."

"That reminds me of the swallows I enjoyed watching when I lived in Ohio," she said, even now envisioning the pretty, sleek-feathered little birds and the grace with which they soared against the darkening heavens each evening at dusk. "The swallows sweep down and around as they catch bugs before going to their nests for the night."

She laughed softly. "I recall one nest of swallows that had been built in the corner beams of our porch in Ohio," she murmured. "I even watched the babies grow and be fed by their parents until they flew from the nest. It was great fun watching the parents teach the grown babies how to fly and how to catch bugs for themselves."

"I know of swallows," Soaring Hawk said as he leaned closer to the fire and slid a log into its flames. "They are sisters to the nighthawks."

"That is so beautiful," Misshi sighed.

Then she turned and faced Soaring Hawk. "Your name is Soaring Hawk," she murmured. "Were you named that because of the nighthawks in this area? Was your mother or father entranced by these birds?"

"My parents never felt one way or another about the nighthawks," Soaring Hawk said, again watching those that were still catching bugs overhead. "Not until one evening, that is."

"What changed their minds?" Misshi asked, eyes wide as she glanced again at the birds.

"It was told to me by my mother when I was old enough to ask questions. When my mother was giving birth to me, the sky seemed unusually filled with nighthawks," Soaring Hawk said. "There were so many that night. They soared and soared. Their strange cries were multiplied, and continued long into the night. Hawks are not known to stay in the heavens very long after the sky becomes totally dark, but these hawks continued to swoop down over my parents' tepee far into the night. My mother and my father saw it as a sign and agreed that I should be named after those birds that had shared my parents' vigil on the night of my mother's long labor. I was told that as I breathed out my first cry, the birds seemed to suddenly vanish into thin air. *Huh*, it was a sign my parents could not ignore. Thus I am called Soaring Hawk."

Suddenly, as though by magic, the birds were gone. Except for the occasional hoot of an owl, or the distant howl of a wolf, the world had gone quiet.

"This night is magical," Misshi murmured. She motioned with a hand toward the sky. "Look at how many stars are in the heavens tonight. It seems far more than usual. The North Star. See how it shines so much more brightly tonight?"

"In Shoshone and Bannock the North Star is called *Wa-se-a-ure-chah-pe*," Soaring Hawk said. "And then there is the Ursa Major which is also called the Seven Stars and The Wagon. It makes its revolution around the polar star, pointing toward it. This is the secret of how my people travel by night when there is no moon."

"I love the Milky Way," Misshi said, gazing at its great cluster of white. "I love how it is called the *moch-pa-achon-ka-hoo*, the 'backbone of the sky.' "

"*Huh*, it is said to mimic the arch of the heavens, and to be as necessary to its support as the backbone of any animal to its body," Soaring Hawk said. "We also believe the Aurora Borealis is a cloud of fire."

167

Without further words, Soaring Hawk drew Mis-shi against him.

As his blanket fell from his shoulders, he swept hers aside, then gently slid her beneath him and gave her a kiss that caused a sensual melting to begin within her all over again.

They came together, their bodies rocking and swaying, as again they made sweet, passionate love.

Elsewhere, far from where Misshi and Soaring Hawk were having their night of love, many eyes gazed down from a bluff onto many darkened te-pees. There were no sounds except for an occasional whinny from a horse corralled behind a tepee.

The green eyes of one man searched until he found the sentries that guarded the stronghold of Chief Bear and his people.

Then he slid his sharp knife from its sheath and nodded to those who were with him to ready their weapons. He had decided not to wait until later to seek out this stronghold and he had found it much more easily than he would have believed possible. He was so close to claiming his sister. How could he wait? He would not even wait until sunrise to attack. The killing would begin now!

Chapter Fifteen

Doubt thou the stars are fire;
Doubt that the sun doth move;
Doubt truth to be a liar;
But never doubt I love.
                    —Shakespeare
                    "Hamlet," Act II

Misshi awakened and immediately saw that Soaring Hawk was no longer in the blankets with her.

Now aware of what seemed to be a slowly swirling cloud of fog coming from high in the mountains, she leaned on an elbow and looked for Soaring Hawk.

When she finally spotted him amid the swirling

grayness, she saw that he was already dressed. He had even readied his horse for travel.

"Soaring Hawk?" Misshi asked, slowly rubbing sleep from her eyes. "What's wrong? You seem anxious to leave."

Soaring Hawk came and knelt beside her. "Do you see it?" he asked. He cast a quick glance over his shoulder and then again peered at Misshi with troubled eyes. "Do you smell it?"

"I think I see fog, and fog has no smell," she said.

But as her senses became more alert, she did detect a faint scent of smoke.

"What you see is not fog," Soaring Hawk said stiffly. "It is smoke that has been filtered by the fresh, cool mountain air."

"What do you think could be on fire?" Misshi asked. She rushed to her feet and hurried into her clothes.

As she brushed her fingers through her hair to comb out the tangles, she watched how frantically Soaring Hawk was rolling up the blankets, and placed them in the bags on the back of his horse. Then just as quickly he kicked dirt onto the campfire, extinguishing it.

Soaring Hawk could hardly hide the terrible fear that had gripped his insides the moment he realized this was smoke, and that it could be coming from his very own stronghold.

Seeing that Misshi was ready to travel, he reached for her hand. "We can see better from the nearby ridge," he said, taking her quickly to her horse.

He helped her into her saddle, then mounted his own steed.

With one kick of their heels they rode away from their campsite.

When they reached the ridge that gave them a full view of the mountain range, Soaring Hawk realized that the point of origination of the fire was not his stronghold after all.

But discovering this did not bring him much relief. His father's stronghold was on the exact opposite side of the mountain from his.

Now it seemed that someone else had discovered it, and had surely gone there during the night, leaving death and destruction behind. There was no doubt that this fire was coming from his father's stronghold.

Something grabbed at his heart.

His mother!

Oh, surely his mother lay dead even now where wolves and other four-legged creatures, as well as dreaded vultures, could feast on her body.

"Soaring Hawk, please tell me," Misshi said, seeing his agony as he gazed in the direction of the fire. "Is it your stronghold? Has someone found it and . . . and—"

"*Ka*, it is not mine," Soaring Hawk said, interrupting her. He turned his eyes to her. "It is my father's."

"Your . . . father's?" Misshi gulped out, her eyes widening. "How would you know? I thought you didn't know where it was."

"I have never specifically said that I do not know where it is. I avoid the lie. I just shrug off the question when it comes my way, for you see, it was my intent to keep my knowledge of my father's stronghold to myself until it was necessary to reveal it," Soaring Hawk said. "I always hoped to be able to confront my father first, alone, to see if I could talk sense into him. Also, I wanted a chance to see my mother again before . . ."

He swallowed hard and hung his head. "*Huh*, until recently I held on to some hope of working things out with my father without interference from anyone else. But when the atrocities worsened and worsened and I thought my father was responsible for them all, I knew there was no hope for him. I knew he would have to be stopped and taken by force, and by many, not only by Soaring Hawk."

He lifted his eyes when he felt Misshi's hands

on his cheeks. "I was so wrong to wait," he said, his voice breaking. "Those who are spreading death and destruction have now attacked my father and mother's people. Surely now they are both dead. Surely all who lived at the stronghold are dead."

"But don't you see, Soaring Hawk, the very fact that your father's stronghold was attacked proves that your father has not been guilty of all those terrible things," Misshi said, dropping her hands from his face. "Someone else is guilty too."

Then her face drained of color. She shook her head slowly back and forth. "No, oh, Lord, surely not," she said. "Oh, surely my brother could not have done this. . . ."

"Yes, he could be the one who is responsible," Soaring Hawk said in a low hiss.

He looked toward the billowing smoke, smoke that he had no doubt was coming from his father's stronghold, for no other village was established in that exact spot.

"I have a terrible feeling that no one's life was spared at my father's stronghold," Soaring Hawk said, his voice breaking with emotion. "My cousins, my aunts, my friends' parents and sisters and brothers . . ."

Tears streamed from Misshi's eyes as she gave Soaring Hawk a look that showed her understanding of his feelings.

He nodded. "Come," he said. "We must continue onward. Soon we shall know the worst of this latest atrocity."

They rode off in silence, Misshi now riding behind him as the path became steeper and narrower. Misshi could see the desperation with which Soaring Hawk was urging his horse onward, and she understood. He must get to his father's stronghold to see if it had been attacked, and whether there were any survivors.

And she even understood why he had not stopped to consider that perhaps he should gathered up a war party before traveling to the sight of another massacre.

Blinded by his eagerness to see if either his mother or father were alive, he had not even thought that he and Misshi might be ambushed.

And she wouldn't remind him that they might possibly become another notch on the murderer's belt. If she did, he would suddenly think of her and the danger he was putting her in. He might even stop and take her back home!

But she didn't want him to do that. If he took the time to escort her safely home, he might arrive at his father's stronghold too late to help some innocent person.

She said a silent prayer that at least his mother's life would have been spared, for from all that Soaring Hawk had said about her, she was a loving woman who had done what was best for her son, even though doing it had condemned her in her husband's eyes.

Misshi wondered if Soaring Hawk had ever thought about the possibility that his mother had been banished from the stronghold for what she had done.

Soon many questions would be answered, for the stench of the smoke was growing stronger and stronger. Misshi covered her mouth and nose with a hand to keep from smelling it, for combined with the smoke was the scent of death.

Chapter Sixteen

Life in common among people
who love each other is the ideal . . . of happiness!
—George Sand

"I built this stockade just for you," Major Dale
Bradley said darkly as he stood clutching the bars
of the cell that held Dale's prized prisoner.

He glared at his prisoner. "You murdering bastard," he growled. "Each bar that I helped install
was a labor of love for me, because I knew that
somehow I would find you and imprison you before
strangling you with my bare hands."

Dale couldn't help being unnerved by the old
chief. He'd came out of the ambush last night

without even a scratch, and now sat stoically on the floor of the cell, his legs crossed, his eyes rarely blinking as he stared ahead at what seemed blank space.

Ever since Dale had captured Chief Bear, the old renegade had not uttered a sound.

Even back at the burning stronghold, Chief Bear had only stared blankly ahead as his wife was taken from his side and shoved with the rest of the women and children.

Dale hadn't killed the women and children during this raid.

He had left them alive for a purpose, to die a slow death on the mountainside, for without their husbands and fathers to hunt food, or horses to travel, they could not survive.

And even knowing this, the old chief still hadn't uttered a sound. He offered no plea of mercy for the women and children. He uttered no outcry of despair when he was taken down the mountain without them.

Nonetheless, Dale gloated over the success of the ambush. Not only had he and his men captured the old chief, they had also captured the sub-chief, Panther Eyes.

Panther Eyes lay in a separate cell, unconscious from a bullet wound in his chest.

Dale had no pity for the young renegade.

He would let the younger Indian die slowly and painfully.

Dale thought he deserved no better than that. Other redskin warriors from the stronghold, young and old alike, filled the other cells, some wounded, others downhearted and wailing prayers to their *Wakonda*.

The more Dale stood there watching the old chief, the more he felt as though Chief Bear was purposely doing this to take away Dale's superiority . . . his elation at having stopped the worst of the Indian renegades.

It would be so easy for Dale to open the barred door, to place his hands around the old chief's thin neck and squeeze the life out of the savage.

That would finally stop the staring.

That would rid the world of one more savage, who to Dale was the worst of the lot.

But Dale had decided that if the old chief wanted to play mind games, so be it. Dale was the best of players.

He could wait for the old man to break down and talk. Dale had had a lifetime of waiting to find the man who stole away his sister so long ago. He could most certainly wait awhile longer.

Dale's only regret was that no one could, or would, tell him the fate of his Misshi.

But neither had he seen a scalp on any of the scalp poles in Chief Bear's stronghold that had the same color hair as his sister's.

Perhaps she had escaped the old man. Perhaps she was alive out there somewhere, living a happy, normal life, even married with children.

But Dale had quit fooling himself long ago that he would ever see Misshi again. He had accepted her loss, but never with a peaceful heart.

And even though he had caught the man he was after, Dale wouldn't stop killing redskins. He was already thinking about his next attack . . . how he would do it, and how he would laugh over the dead bodies!

He was thinking that he would like to find Chief Soaring Hawk's stronghold. Ah, now wouldn't *that* be a challenge. It was said that no one knew where Soaring Hawk had established his stronghold.

Dale decided that he would follow the young chief to his stronghold, then return with his men and wipe out the entire village.

Dale had loathed Soaring Hawk the instant he met him. Yes, the young Bannock chief had to die!

"Washakie as well," Dale whispered. He was tired of being told to leave Washakie alone.

No one bossed Major Dale Bradley around, es-

pecially not that prim and proper Colonel Braddock at Fort Bridger.

"Not even the President of these United States."
He laughed, his eyes shining with an evil glint.

Chapter Seventeen

Live while ye may,
Ye happy pair.
                —Milton

Morning had turned to noon.

Soaring Hawk and Misshi had stopped and made a quick meal of berries, *chau-sho-sha*, red willow, *chint-nah*, wild grapes, and raw fish.

They had then proceeded upward, the smell of smoke growing stronger the farther they traveled up the mountainside. Misshi spotted a herd of antelope standing together, grazing. The wind was blowing from their direction toward Misshi and Soaring Hawk, so the animals did not scent them.

Cassie Edwards

For just an instant the animals stood there; then, like a flash, they wheeled as though executing a military maneuver, and with seemingly effortless jumps the graceful creatures glided away like phantoms.

The path was narrow and steep now, bordered by a rocky stream that occasionally became a waterfall splashing down the mountain.

The sun was now waning as the smoke thickened. Misshi and Soaring Hawk both suffered from stinging eyes, and dry, aching throats as they breathed it.

But still they prodded their steeds onward. The horses were suffering from the smoke as well, and would occasionally shake their heads back and forth and neigh nervously.

Misshi ached from head to toe. She wasn't sure she could go on.

Yet she couldn't find the words to tell Soaring Hawk. She knew he had to learn what had happened. In his eyes she could see the pain of knowing what they might find when they reached the stronghold.

His mother had surely not lived through the ordeal. Most, or all, of the people he'd known had probably perished.

She wanted to ask Soaring Hawk again just how much farther they had to go to reach their destination, but realized that it had not been long since she had already asked him. And she vowed to herself not to mention it again, for he was deep in thought.

She wondered if he was reliving times long past, when he had been a child who had been aware of the demon his father was. She wondered if he was remembering being held in his mother's arms as she sang to him.

Misshi could understand his sadness. All she had to do was think of how happy and content her own family had been before heading out with the wagon train from Ohio, and she would be filled with longing.

She was assailed by memories of her brother and how kind he had been. She could see him now as he ran through the knee-high grasses with Misshi, holding her hand. They caught butterflies, then set them free. They caught lightning bugs, placing them in jars for only a little while to enjoy their magical glow, but it had always been Dale who would hurriedly set them free because he did not want any to die.

Yes, back then Dale had been so sweet, so compassionate . . .

Misshi was brought out of her thoughts by a movement up ahead.

She stiffened and peered harder into the smoke.

She thought she heard something like children crying.

And then again she heard it.

Her heart skipped a beat, for she now knew that what she had heard *was* the sound of children sobbing. She also heard soft wailing of women.

"Soaring Hawk . . ." Misshi said, looking quickly at him. "I heard . . ."

Soaring Hawk's heart was hammering inside his chest as he peered more intently into the swirling smoke. "I also heard . . ."

His words faded as both he and Misshi suddenly saw one child, then two, then women, and many, many more children emerge from the smoke like ghosts.

They were stumbling and clinging to one another, their ash-covered faces revealing terrible pain.

Expecting to see someone herding the children and women down the mountain like cattle, Soaring Hawk drew his rifle from its gunboot and took aim to kill the guilty party the moment he spied them.

But Misshi forgot the danger.

She leaped from her horse and ran to the children. She fell to her knees and gathered as many as she could into her arms. Others clustered around her, reaching out for her, begging for help.

Soaring Hawk rode around her and the children, but when he saw there were no men with the women and children, he dismounted.

As the women clustered around him, as his gaze moved eagerly over their smoke-blackened faces, searching out his mother.

His heart skipped a beat as the eyes of one of the women arrested his attention.

It was the intense look in those eyes that he remembered so well. His mother's face had changed. She was thin, frail, wrinkled, and worn-out looking, but her eyes were the same.

And though she looked tired, she was not ill. It seemed that the report about her illness had been a ploy to lure him to her, surely to be killed the instant he stepped inside his father's stronghold.

White Snow Feather was filled with joy as she suddenly recognized the warrior who stood there so closely scrutinizing her.

Huh, she knew her Soaring Hawk at once. He was the exact image of her husband as a young man. It was as though time had been turned back and Bear was again that young man who had courted her, then wed her.

Ah, when their one and only child was born, what pride she had seen in her husband's eyes. She had hoped that the birth of a son would change her husband's life, that it would make him forget his hate, his need of vengeance against whites.

But, no. Nothing could mitigate the anger born inside him the day soldiers came in the dark of night and killed most of Bear's people.

His mother and father were among those who had died that day. Also his cousins . . . his grandparents.

Ka, nothing had stopped his hate until that bullet entered the base of his skull and rendered him almost a vegetable.

But that was all in the past now. Even her husband was a memory, for surely he would soon die the worst death of all for a proud red man: while incarcerated by white soldiers.

She was glad now that he would not know the disgrace, for Chief Bear would not even be conscious of these last worst days of his life.

With tears falling from her eyes, White Snow Feather ran to Soaring Hawk and flung herself into his arms.

He held her close, wincing when he felt her bones through her flesh, and smelled the stench of death in her scorched gray hair.

Misshi's eyes filled with tears when she heard Soaring Hawk murmur, "Mother." Miracle of miracles, his mother was alive.

Misshi looked past the women and children, into the swirling smoke. She only now realized that no men were traveling with the group.

Who had committed this atrocity? Where was Chief Bear? Where were his warriors?

Had they all been killed?

Misshi didn't want to hope that Bear was dead, although she knew it would be a loss mourned by few.

For Soaring Hawk's sake, she hoped that Bear was alive. She knew Soaring Hawk wanted a chance to make some sort of peace with him.

For a moment, Misshi just stood and watched Soaring Hawk and his mother, who seemed afraid to let go of each other. Then she put her arms around him from behind as he continued to embrace his mother.

Misshi's heart went out to him. For so long he had been denied his mother's love. She would do everything in her power to make sure he was never denied her own love.

Chapter Eighteen

Come live with me, and be my love;
And we will all the pleasures prove
That valleys, groves, hills, and fields,
Woods, or steepy mountain yields.
—Christopher Marlowe

Soaring Hawk and Misshi had led his mother and
the other women and children to a creek where
they had refreshed themselves. The black ash had
been removed from their faces, but their clothes
and hair still reeked of it.

The women and children now sat all around
Soaring Hawk, his mother, and Misshi as White
Snow Feather talked in a low, quivering voice

about what had happened at their stronghold.

Soaring Hawk clutched his mother's hand as he listened. He hated those who were responsible for this latest travesty, yet he was grateful that the women and children's lives had been spared.

He was thankful that he was able to hold his mother's hand, when he might have been readying her body for its grave.

Misshi looked slowly around the circle at the women and children and the deep sadness etched onto their faces. Their lives had been spared, but surely ruined. They would be haunted forever by the sight of loved ones murdered before their very eyes.

Misshi vowed to herself that she would do everything possible to help them. They could not be held accountable for what their renegade husbands and fathers had done.

And since Misshi was going to marry Soaring Hawk soon, she would request that these women and children come to live among his people. Misshi would make it her goal to put sunshine back in their eyes. It was surely meant to be her mission in life.

Her eyes were drawn back to White Snow Feather as the older woman continued telling about the events that led up to the ambush, and then the ambush itself.

"It was such a peaceful evening before the ambush," White Snow Feather said, her voice breaking. "The sun was a beautiful orange disc in the sky as it began setting behind the highest peak of the mountain last night. All of our children gathered around, outside beside the communal fire, and listened to tales told by our storyteller, tales told since the beginning of time which make one laugh and dream."

She paused, swallowed hard, then continued. "It was easy to forget that Panther Eyes and the young, fiercest warriors of our village were gathered in the council house making plans for their next murderous raid."

"Panther Eyes, my father's right-hand man, his sub-chief," Soaring Hawk said, recalling a renegade whose eyes had been filled with evil. "And so he has lived through the raids. *Huh*, he would. Someone as driven as he, would."

As though she hadn't heard him, White Snow Feather continued. "Yes, before going to bed, stories were told and the elder warriors gathered to smoke pipes and relive the exploits of their past," she said. "It was a good night. There was, for a while, a sense of normalcy in our village, as though none of our warriors were plotting against others. The stories were good. The laughter was sweet."

She hung her head in her hands and began to

sob. "When everyone went to bed, hearts were warm and happy," she said. "Then suddenly there was gunfire, screams, wails, and fire everywhere as the soldiers who came like evil spirits in the night set our lodges aflame, leaving all but a few men wounded or dead. The children and women were gathered together outside their burning lodges, crying and clinging as we awaited our fate. All expected to die, but the head soldier—we heard his men call him Major Bradley—gave the order to let the women and children go."

She raised her eyes and peered at her son. "This Major Bradley gave the order to let the women and children go, to let us die as we tried to reach help on foot. The soldiers had already released all of the horses and sent them away. They took as prisoners the surviving men, including Panther Eyes, who was severely wounded."

White Snow Feather dipped her head low and rested her face in her hands as she became too emotional to go on.

Her body shook with sobs.

The other women joined in a low chanting, as a way to show their sympathy for their chief's wife.

Misshi was in a state of shock. Her heart seemed to have stopped dead inside her at the mention of her brother's name. She had never, deep down inside herself, believed her brother could do such cruel things. But now she knew.

"Mother, what of my father?" Soaring Hawk asked. "Mother, what was my father's fate at the hands of the soldiers?"

Misshi scarcely breathed as she watched his mother wipe her eyes then lift them and meet the questioning in her son's. "Your father was taken alive," she said solemnly. "There were no wounds this night. But the wound he received many summers ago has rendered him almost helpless."

Helpless? Soaring Hawk could not envision a man as powerful and muscled as his father being helpless. It would be a thing worse than death for such a man as Chief Bear!

"Mother, just how long has it been since father was wounded?" Soaring Hawk asked.

"Many, many summers ago," White Snow Feather said, a sob lodging in her throat. "Yes, it was on the day of one of your father's raids against a white man's wagon train, on the day you left our stronghold, on the day your father took captive a white girl with hair the color of the sunset. A white man's bullet entered the base of your father's skull, but it did not kill him. Only that part of him that gave him the ability to think died that day. He has not been in charge of his life, or his people, since."

Soaring Hawk was stunned by his mother's words. His father had been wounded on the very day of Soaring Hawk's exit from Chief Bear's life?

He glanced quickly at Misshi, whose eyes were wide. He knew she had never realized how badly Chief Bear was wounded as she fled from him.

A new thought struck Soaring Hawk. His father could not possibly have been responsible for all the atrocities that had been laid at his door all these years.

"Mother, if Father was so disabled, then who has been responsible for the raids, the trail of blood that my father was being blamed for?" he asked.

"Panther Eyes," White Snow Feather said quickly. "Panther Eyes was in charge. He is responsible for all the atrocities blamed on your father these past ten winters and summers."

She reached over and clutched Soaring Hawk's arm. "Son, I could never leave the stronghold to tell anyone of my husband's innocence. I have been a prisoner. Your father has been a prisoner. All of my people, except for those warriors who allied themselves with Panther Eyes, have been prisoners of a deranged man who spread violence in the name of Chief Bear. Panther Eyes had said that if he was ever captured, he would plead for his own life by saying that he was forced to do the killings by his deranged chief, while in truth, he did it all because killing is in his blood. He who claims to be so powerful is in truth a low-down, stinking coward."

She sighed heavily. "But the reign of terror is now over," she murmured. "Panther Eyes has been taken captive by the soldiers. And he cannot plead his case, nor cast blame on my husband for the wrongs he himself did to mankind. He was severely injured and might even be dead by now."

Her fingers dug even more deeply into Soaring Hawk's arm. "*Mea!* Go! Save your father," she cried. "He is not guilty of all he has been accused of. He does not deserve to pay for what others have done. And surely those incarcerated Bannock warriors who might tell the truth will soon die and the truth about their chief will go to the grave with them."

Sobbing, she continued. "Your father is not able to speak for himself. He has not spoken a word since he was first wounded. I am afraid that the soldiers will make your father die slowly . . . painfully, because of the massacres carried out by Panther Eyes and his followers. Of course, everyone knows that my husband was responsible for much cruelty and death in his younger years. But these past ten winters he has done nothing wrong. Surely being incapacitated in this way is payment enough for his past transgressions. He deserves pity now, not incarceration by whites and the punishments they will lay upon him."

She again squeezed her fingers into his arm. "Please, Soaring Hawk, go and see that your father is released before it is too late."

Misshi had listened to everything and was now catapulted back to that day when so many had died at the hand of Chief Bear and his renegade warriors.

Afraid her emotions would cause her to say the wrong thing to this distraught old woman, Misshi rushed to her feet and ran away from them, to be alone with her thoughts.

Soaring Hawk's heart skipped a beat when he saw Misshi leave, yet he understood her departure. He had noticed how quiet she had become while listening to his mother. Surely when his mother had begged for mercy for her husband, a man who had slain so many of Misshi's friends, it was hard for her to take.

How could she want mercy for such a man?

He pulled his arm free of his mother's grip and leaped to his feet to go after Misshi, but his mother moved to her feet as well and stood in his way.

Her eyes searched his face. "Who is this woman who is dressed like an Indian, yet who is obviously white?" she asked softly. "Why is this woman with you, my son?"

Soaring Hawk saw no choice but to reveal the truth immediately.

He placed gentle hands on his mother's frail shoulders.

"Mother, the woman's name is Misshi," he said, looking past White Snow Feather and seeing that Misshi had stopped and was sitting in the shadows of trees. As soon as he explained to his mother, he would go to Misshi and try to make things right for her as well.

"Mother, this is the girl with hair the color of the sunset whom my father abducted during his last raid," he said thickly. "While Father lay wounded on the ground, she managed to escape. She has since lived among the Shoshone. She has been adopted by Chief Washakie. She is now more Shoshone than white. She even dyed her hair to look Shoshone. In her heart, she is one of us."

White Snow Feather stepped away from Soaring Hawk.

She turned slowly, then stopped and stared at the white woman whose path had briefly crossed her own so long ago.

This woman had fled before White Snow Feather had known anything about her, but she had been told later by Panther Eyes all about the entrancing white girl with hair of flame, how she had been abducted by Chief Bear, and then about how she had escaped their stronghold.

White Snow Feather watched Soaring Hawk hurry to the woman he called Misshi and pull her up into his arms.

Fear clutched White Snow Feather's heart. She was afraid that this white woman would keep Soaring Hawk from going to help his father. From the way he held her in his arms, it was obvious they were more than traveling companions. They were in love.

White Snow Feather now doubted that Soaring Hawk would go to rescue his father. His woman must hate Chief Bear with all of her heart and would surely stand in the way.

A keen resentment of Misshi was born at that moment inside White Snow Feather's heart.

Chapter Nineteen

Sweetheart, come see if the rose
Which at morning began to unclose
Its damask gown to the sun
Has not lost, now the day is done,
The folds of its damasked gown
And its colors so like your own.
—Ronsard

The sound of horses climbing the steep path caused the refugees to fall silent.

Soaring Hawk and Misshi gave each other a look of alarm.

"Can the soldiers be returning?" Misshi whispered, her heart thundering in her chest. "Soaring

201

Hawk, do you think Dale changed his mind and . . . and . . . decided to return to the stronghold to kill those he left behind?"

Soaring Hawk looked quickly at the women and children, whose eyes were wide with fear as they watched for the arrival of those who were approaching.

He felt a deep sadness to think that he had not arrived in time to help his mother's people. If he and Misshi had not stopped that one time to eat, perhaps he would have found these people earlier. Perhaps he could have found shelter for them by now where they could hide from those who wished them dead.

Misshi hurried over to the refugees. "Come to me," she said, reaching her hands out for the women and children. She motioned toward them. "Draw together in a tight circle around me. Hold hands. And . . . be . . . brave. Soaring Hawk is here. He will do what he can to protect you."

She watched Soaring Hawk grab his rifle from the gunboot at the side of his horse as the women and children moved into a tight circle around her, their hands clasped.

Misshi felt the trembling of the hands that held hers and understood the refugees' fear. She hoped that they felt some comfort when Soaring Hawk stepped protectively in front of them, his rifle ready.

Everyone's breath quickened as the horses grew closer and closer. They were so near now, those waiting could hear the horses' labored breathing from the hard trek up the mountainside.

When the lead rider came into view, Soaring Hawk's eyes widened and his whole body relaxed. He felt a rush of joyous relief when he saw that the man in the lead, riding a midnight black stallion, was his best friend. It was Lone Wolf.

Following closely in single file behind Lone Wolf were many of Soaring Hawk's warriors.

Lone Wolf came closer, then dismounted and gazed questioningly at the clinging women and children.

"Lone Wolf," Soaring Hawk said happily. He held his rifle to his side as he embraced Lone Wolf with his free arm. "I have never been happier to see you."

Lone Wolf returned the embrace, then eased back from Soaring Hawk. "I see so many here that I remember from childhood," he said, looking from woman to woman.

Both his mother and father had died long before Lone Wolf had left the stronghold with Soaring Hawk. Being without any relatives who lived among those people he had left behind, he had no one to search out among those who were now eagerly watching the other arriving warriors.

Lone Wolf looked over his shoulder at the men who were dismounting quickly and running to loved ones they recognized.

Mothers and sons were reunited.

Aunts, cousins, and sisters ran to the warriors and clung and cried.

Misshi covered her mouth with a hand and stifled an emotional sob brought on by the joy etched on so many faces. She went and stood on one side of Soaring Hawk while his mother stood on the other, as the reunions continued and tears were mixed with laughter.

"It is good to see," Soaring Hawk said, his voice husky with his own deep-felt emotion. He had known how many years his warriors had longed to see their families again. Most had doubted they ever would.

He looked quickly at Lone Wolf. "How is it that you are on this side of the mountain when we never travel here?" he asked, drawing Lone Wolf's eyes to his.

"From the high bluffs where they watch for intruders, our posted sentries saw the smoke and alerted me to it," Lone Wolf said. "We followed the smoke to find its source." He paused, then raised an eyebrow. "My chief, did you come to investigate the smoke also?"

"Yes, that is so," Soaring Hawk said, nodding. "I was bringing my woman to our stronghold. I was bringing my Misshi, the woman I am soon to wed."

Lone Wolf gazed at Misshi, then looked questioningly at Soaring Hawk.

"No, I have not mentioned her to you," Soaring Hawk said, lifting a hand to Lone Wolf's shoulder. "I have not known her for long, but it was our destiny to meet, love, and marry. In time, when you know Misshi, you will see how one can love a woman so quickly."

"She is half-breed?" Lone Wolf asked bluntly. "You would marry a half-breed?"

"She is not half-breed, she is white," Soaring Hawk said, knowing his other warriors and their families would have the same question. "She is white, but raised Shoshone. She is Washakie's adopted daughter."

Soaring Hawk dropped his hand to his side. "We will talk more later," he said. "Now my focus must be elsewhere. I am sure you understand."

"*Huh*, and I am sorry that I have delayed you," Lone Wolf said. "I apologize, my chief."

"Apologies are never needed between us," Soaring Hawk said. "Lone Wolf, you came at a time when I was filled with worry about how to get these women and children to safety. I did not see how it was possible with only two horses. These women and children cannot travel much farther on foot. They are worn out. Many are weak."

Then Soaring Hawk smiled. "My friend, you were sent to me by the spirits. You were sent with your horses so that these women and children will have a way to travel to our stronghold, for that is where I have chosen to take them. Our stronghold is much closer than Washakie's village. It is best to get the women and children where they can get food, baths, clean clothes, and a place to recover from the nightmare of these past hours."

"I will instruct several warriors to build travois for the trip to our stronghold," Lone Wolf said, hurrying away.

Misshi hugged Soaring Hawk. "It is not only a miracle that Lone Wolf came today, but also that *we* were led here," she murmured.

She went with him and helped make the travois. Limbs were cut from trees, and then smaller branches were tied across them with pliable willow switches.

Soon several travois were ready to transport the most elderly women.

The other, healthier, stronger women and the children joined the warriors on their horses, now ready for the journey to the other side of the mountain.

Soaring Hawk helped his mother onto the travois that had been attached to Lone Wolf's steed. Soaring Hawk gazed with love at his mother, then nodded with the affection of a best friend at Lone Wolf.

"See to the safety of our people, Lone Wolf," Soaring Hawk said. "Duty calls me elsewhere. Duty to my father."

Soaring Hawk gazed lovingly at his mother again. "Mother, I will do what I can to reunite you and Father," he said. "I will gain my father's freedom and then bring him to you. As for Panther Eyes? If he is still alive, he will remain with the soldiers to pay for his crimes."

"My son, do you believe that your father has already paid for his crimes?" she asked, her voice breaking. "He lives the life of a mindless one. Please bring him to me. He still has my love and devotion. He . . . knows . . . nothing but that, my son. I believe that is the only reason he is still alive."

"Yes, I do believe that Father has paid his dues," Soaring Hawk said, nodding. "And know this, Mother, your husband, my father, still has his son's love and devotion, too."

White Snow Feather's eyes wavered as she gazed

at Misshi. "What of her, Soaring Hawk?" she asked. "Will she allow this helpless old man his freedom? Can she forgive enough not to stand in the way of such freedom?"

Misshi turned toward White Snow Feather. She tried to ignore the resentment in the depths of the woman's eyes.

"White Snow Feather," Misshi said, "I can never forget what Chief Bear did to my family, and I'm not sure I can ever forgive him, but if Soaring Hawk can bargain for his release, I will not interfere."

Just that quickly, the antagonism White Snow Feather had felt for Misshi was gone. Her heart warmed toward this young woman whose life had been irrevocably altered by the actions of her renegade husband.

Now it even seemed right that Soaring Hawk would meet this woman and love her. The fact that she was born white did not trouble the old woman, for in all ways that mattered, Misshi had become Shoshone.

In that respect it seemed that White Snow Feather's husband had done this woman a service, for who would not want to be Shoshone . . . or Bannock, for that matter?

And if the girl had not been abducted by Chief

Bear, she would never have met such a man as Soaring Hawk.

White Snow Feather reached out for Misshi's hand and took it in hers as Misshi knelt down beside the travois. "Thank you," she said, tears shining in her eyes. "You have made this old woman happy." She slid a slow smile over at Soaring Hawk. "As I see you have made this old woman's son happy." She held her son's gaze for a moment, then looked again at Misshi. "I welcome you inside my heart."

Misshi was touched deeply when White Snow Feather suddenly swept her thin, frail arms around her in a tender hug, then sighed as she lay back on the blankets covering the travois.

Misshi took a blanket from one of Soaring Hawk's bags and gently, lovingly spread it over White Snow Feather, up to her chin.

Smiling, she dipped low and kissed White Snow Feather on her cheek, then gazed into the old, faded eyes and said, "I welcome you, also, inside my heart."

They embraced; then Misshi stood away as Soaring Hawk gave his mother another fond hug.

Soaring Eagle and Misshi stood hand in hand as the procession began toward Soaring Hawk's stronghold.

Soaring Hawk suddenly reached for Misshi and

drew her into his embrace. He held her close. "My woman, I am so blessed to have found you," he murmured, then stepped away from her and helped her onto her horse. "I shall love you forever."

"As I shall love you," Misshi said.

She smiled as he mounted his steed. She was trying so hard not to think about what lay ahead . . . the unavoidable meeting with the man who had brought such sadness and heartache into her life.

Also, Misshi would meet her brother face to face for the first time since that fateful day. This would *not* be a reunion of the heart. It would be one of pain and unhappiness.

She knew that she would not be able to keep herself from hating Dale for what he had turned into . . . a man whose heart had gone bad.

Chapter Twenty

When I behold, upon the night's starr'd face,
High cloudy symbols of a high romance.
                                    —John Keats

The fire was burning low in Washakie's lodge. The mood was somber as Soaring Hawk and Misshi sat with her adoptive father beside the fire.

Soaring Hawk had just finished telling Washakie about the ambush at his father's stronghold, and about who was responsible.

"It is all so wrong," Washakie said as he drew a blanket more snugly around his shoulders. "And I cannot understand why Major Bradley pretended not to know where Chief Bear's stronghold was. It must be that he was planning this raid all along."

He frowned at Soaring Hawk. "It is as we feared," he said flatly. "This major, who is new in the area, is not a man to trust. He should have worked with us in taking Chief Bear captive. Colonel Harry Braddock at Fort Bridger should also have been involved."

"In the white man's eyes, Major Bradley will not be judged as having broken any laws by doing this on his own, but there is one thing that no one knew before he raided my father's stronghold," Soaring Hawk said tightly. "There is something about all of this that no one was aware of."

"That is?" Washakie said, raising an eyebrow.

"Major Bradley holds prisoner an old chief who has not been a part of any murder or mayhem for these past ten winters," Soaring Hawk said. His heart ached anew to think of his father's condition. "The atrocities that were blamed on my father were, in truth, the work of his sub-chief."

"What do you mean?" Washakie asked, leaning closer.

He glanced at Misshi, who sat at Soaring Hawk's right side, silent and full of thought as she stared into the fire. He knew she had always wanted to learn the fate of her brother, and now that she knew, and had discovered that he had such hatred for the red man, her pride in her brother must have suffered a terrible blow.

Washakie felt a deep sympathy for what Misshi must be feeling now.

Soaring Hawk drew Washakie's eyes back to him as he solemnly explained about his father's injury.

"My father should no longer be held accountable for any of the atrocities of these past ten winters," Soaring Hawk said. "His mind is gone. He cannot even recall the evil deeds he was responsible for."

Misshi was no longer lost in her own thoughts. Now she was listening intently to Soaring Hawk. She could hear the hurt in his voice as he spoke of his father. She reached over and took his hand and squeezed it gently.

"My father's hours are numbered, because as Major Bradley tries to get answers out of my father—a man who does not remember anything, not even his own name—Major Bradley surely believes my father's silence is caused by stubbornness, not an inability to speak. Major Bradley might go into a fit of rage and kill my father."

"I cannot even imagine Chief Bear as you describe him, so I can see why the major would have trouble believing it," Washakie said dryly. "Yes, we must hurry to the fort and try to reason with Major Bradley."

He paused, kneaded his brow, then sighed. "But,

Soaring Hawk, will the major believe you? Or do you think Major Bradley will think it is a ploy on our part in order to rescue Chief Bear?"

Misshi could stay silent no longer. She stood over them, her eyes filled with determination. "My brother will listen to reason if his own sister is the one telling him the truth about Chief Bear," she said. "Surely Dale will be happy to see me and know that I am alive. That alone might make his mood soften toward the old chief."

She paused, swallowed hard, then said, "And if he sees that I, the one Chief Bear took captive, asks for his release, surely he will decide it is right to do so."

She lowered her eyes. "I doubt that I can tell my brother that I forgive Chief Bear, for I don't think I ever can."

Washakie and Soaring Hawk exchanged quick glances, neither one responding to Misshi. Both were thinking that it was questionable how the major would react to a sister who was now more Indian than white.

"*Huh*, maybe so," Washakie finally responded. "Maybe your brother will be so happy to see you and know that you are alive, he will not react in any way but with joy at finding his long-lost sister. And it is known far and wide that Washakie does not speak with a forked tongue, that what he says

214

is truth. Surely among the three of us, Major Bradley can be convinced to free the ailing chief."

Soaring Hawk rose to his feet. He took Misshi's hands and drew her up beside him. He gazed down at Washakie with eagerness in his eyes. "*Mea-dro,* come. Let us leave now," he said, his heart pounding at the thought that soon he would see his father again.

Washakie stood up and looked from Misshi to Soaring Hawk. "We three will travel alone to Fort Adams," he said. "It is best this way. If we should arrive in numbers at the fort, it might be construed as a planned attack. We might draw fire from the cavalrymen. We are not going there to start a war. We are going there to get your father, and to question this major who took so much on himself and who lied so easily about not knowing where your father's stronghold was."

"I want to think that he did it for the glory of singlehandedly capturing the old chief, not for the thrill of killing those they left behind lying in their life's blood," Misshi said, swallowing hard. "But I cannot help thinking the worst of my brother, for he has proven himself capable of nothing better."

"Perhaps you should not go," Soaring Hawk said as he placed gentle hands on Misshi's cheeks. He framed her face and lifted her eyes to his. "My woman, what we are about to do could be dangerous. Should your brother want to spill more blood—"

Misshi placed a quick hand on Soaring Hawk's mouth, preventing further words that she did not want to hear. "He is surely not so bloodthirsty that he would order us dead before we even got the chance to enter the fort and explain our presence there," she said, her voice breaking.

She lowered her eyes. "I am going to remember the goodness of my brother that I knew as a child," she murmured. "Surely his need for vengeance against those who stole me away from him has not erased all of the good in his heart."

Soaring Hawk drew her into his arms. "You can go with us, for I know that is truly what you need to do," he said. "It is time for you to meet your brother so you can begin to heal. I believe that once you have met him eye to eye, you will need no more convincing about the evil that lies within him. You will see. You will know. Then you will be able to put this man from your mind and from your life, forever. Only after seeing him will the true healing begin inside your heart."

"I wish it were different," Misshi said, tears filling her eyes. "But there is no going back now. What is, is. What was, was. What will be, will be. And the 'will be's' are what I will keep in mind.

It is our future together that will make all of this bearable."

"*Mea-dro*. Let us go now," Washakie said, holding back the entrance flap for Misshi and Soaring Hawk.

Misshi brushed tears from her eyes and nodded.

She left the tepee with Washakie and Soaring Hawk and mounted her steed as they mounted theirs.

Soaring Hawk gave her an easy, reassuring smile. "Misshi, today is only a brief moment in time," he said softly. "Soon it will be tomorrow and tomorrow and then another tomorrow. I vow to you now that I will do everything within my power to see that our tomorrows will all be filled with happiness and joy."

"And *mah-tao-yo's*, little ones?" Misshi asked.

That statement drew Washakie's eyes quickly to her. She felt him looking at her. She turned to him and smiled. "*Huh*, Washakie, you will be a grandfather many times over if Soaring Hawk and I have anything to say, or *do*, about it," she murmured.

She was glad that talking about such things had lightened their mood. Pleasant thoughts would make the moments that lay ahead of them more bearable.

She held her chin high and rode onward between Soaring Hawk and Washakie. She felt that she had already conquered her fear of facing her brother.

How could she be afraid when she had two valorous men to give her their strength and courage to carry with her?

She smiled.

Chapter Twenty-one

The red rose whispers of passion
And the white rose breathes of love;
O, the red rose is a falcon,
And the white rose is a dove.
                    —John Boyle O'Reilly

As she prepared to walk into the office at Fort Adams to face her brother, Misshi grabbed Soaring Hawk's hand for strength. She stopped in surprise when Dale suddenly yanked the door open and stepped out onto the small porch, his fists on his hips as he stared suspiciously at her.

Overwhelmed by emotion at seeing her brother again after so many years, Misshi fought against tears. Her brother was staring at her strangely.

Surely he could see the emotion in her eyes. Surely he recognized her?

She gripped Soaring Hawk's hand more tightly when Dale frowned and stepped down from the porch. He stood directly before Misshi, his eyes scrutinizing her.

She could tell that he did recognize something about her, yet perhaps he did not trust his eyes. He would never have thought to see her dressed as an Indian, proud to look like one.

He would have not expected his sister to be holding an Indian's hand, which proved that she had deep feelings for him.

One part of her wanted to rush into Dale's arms and never let go of him again.

Yet the other part knew that the man he was today was far removed from the young man she remembered. She held herself back, uncertain how to react.

"Hello, big brother," she suddenly blurted out, the words surprising even herself.

She scarcely breathed when she saw his reaction to her words. His eyes grew wide as he took a shaky step away from her.

"What . . . did . . . you say?" he gulped out, his face having gone pale. He visibly shuddered as though what she had said had made him almost physically ill.

"Did you . . . call . . . me your brother?" he gasped out.

"Yes, Dale, you are my *tah-mah*, which in the Shoshone and Bannock language means brother," Misshi said, her voice breaking. "You are my brother. I am Misshi."

She eased her hand from Soaring Hawk's and dared to take a step closer to her brother. "Dale, don't you recognize your own sister?" she said, her voice quivering with strong emotion.

She ran her eyes slowly over Dale and saw how muscular he was and how handsome his cleanly shaven face was, and how good he looked in his buckskin attire.

She had to force tears back when she realized that he was almost the exact image of their father, a man she had idolized and had missed terribly through the years.

"Dale, you look so much like Father," Misshi said shakily, then steadied her voice and straightened her shoulders. She stiffened her upper lip and lifted her chin defiantly.

"But, Dale, that resemblance goes only skin deep, doesn't it?" she said dryly. "Your ideals are vastly different from our father's. There was not one bone in his body that was prejudiced. But . . .

221

I can understand how you could have changed . . .
how you could have taken the wrong road in life.
That day when I was taken away surely made you
change into a bitter, vengeful person, someone
even you might find difficult to recognize if you
would stop and let yourself think about it."

Dale was stunned speechless hearing this woman
speak about him and his family.

Could this be Misshi?

Or was this a ploy?

But to achieve what?

Yet this woman's hair was black. Misshi's had
been such a lovely reddish-gold color.

He looked at her eyes. Ah, yes, they were a
beautiful violet, almost translucent, like Misshi's
had been.

How could two women have the same beautiful
eyes?

But still he could not allow himself to believe
that this woman dressed like an Indian, who held
hands with Chief Soaring Hawk as though they
were in love, could be his sister.

He slid slow eyes over to Chief Washakie, then
looked at Soaring Hawk. He chuckled beneath his
breath as he understood the game being played by
these two redskins. It was because of the old chief
that he held captive in a cell. Washakie and Soaring Hawk had surely come to claim the old chief

and had brought this half-breed woman with them to use as a pawn to him in their possession.

It tore at Dale's heart to think that they would toy with his emotions in this way, that they would pretend this was the sister he had adored.

A keen resentment was building quickly within him toward the two chiefs, and especially toward the woman. He glared at her. "Whatever you are called, you can forget your game and go back to your flea-bitten tepee and think of games to play on someone else," he hissed out bitterly.

He shifted his gaze to Chief Washakie, then glared at Soaring Hawk. "And as for you two chiefs who've decided to take a stand against me, I'm clever enough to know when I am being duped. You'd best forget about having a victory celebration tonight, for I'm not relinquishing my claim on Chief Bear," he said darkly. "I won him fair and square." He chuckled. "Although you two chiefs were born and raised in this area, and should know the lay of the land, it took me, a man from Ohio, to find the old chief's stronghold when no one else could."

He lifted his chin smugly and folded his arms aggressively across his chest. "Yep, it took Major Dale Bradley to stop the old chief's reign of terror," he said. He glared from Soaring Hawk to Washakie. "Now get out of here. Be on your way. Leave

223

me to my glory, to have my *own* celebration."

He glared at Misshi and nodded toward her. "And take this savage squaw, this half-breed, with you," he spat out. "You didn't fool me. This *couldn't* be my sister. She'd never side with savages."

Dale took a slow step closer to Misshi and bent down closer to her face. He raised an eyebrow and kneaded his chin. "No, she'd never have sided with savages," he repeated thickly. "Not unless she was brainwashed into doing it."

Misshi was fighting bitter disappointment in her brother. Not only had he failed to recognize her, but also every word he spoke proved just how prejudiced he was.

She shivered at what he had done back at Chief Bear's stronghold. The looks on the faces of the women and children would be engraved in Misshi's mind forever.

"Dale, you are wrong to think that I was brainwashed into being who I am today," Misshi blurted out. "Dale, I *am* Misshi. I *am* your sister. And I am with Washakie and Soaring Hawk because I wish to be, not because I was forced. And I am not a part of any scam. I have come today not only to help free Chief Bear, but also . . . to . . . meet my brother and let him know that I am alive and well."

For a moment Misshi thought that her words

had hit home. Her brother's eyes were softer in expression as he again closely scrutinized her.

But when he threw his head back in a sudden mocking laugh, Misshi was shaken.

Soaring Hawk took Misshi by the hand and drew her back away from Dale, pulling her protectively close to his side.

When Misshi looked up at Soaring Hawk, tears shone in her eyes. Soaring Hawk knew that he had to make this man understand the truth, for Misshi's sake.

This man did not deserve to know that his beloved sister was alive. Soaring Hawk would like to tell Dale that he was right . . . that Misshi wasn't his sister, and leave it at that.

But Soaring Hawk knew that would never satisfy Misshi.

"Major Bradley, this *is* your *sister*," Soaring Hawk said, his jaw tight.

"And even if you do not recognize anything about me, surely the proof is in my name," Misshi murmured.

"Anyone can copy a name," Dale scoffed. He again placed his fists on his hips. "You aren't my sister. She'd *never* side with the savages who altered her life forever." He laughed scornfully as he glared at her hair. "And look at that hair. Misshi's was the color of mine."

"Like you, people can change, and so can the color of one's hair, as I have changed mine. I dye it black, Dale, to blend in better with the people with whom I live," Misshi said.

She stepped away from Soaring Hawk, bent her neck so that the top of her head was close to Dale, then with her long and slender fingers slowly parted her hair. The roots had begun to grow out since she'd last dyed it, revealing her natural red-gold color.

"Dale, look at the roots of my hair," Misshi said. "Is not that proof enough?"

Dale gasped and took a quick step away from her.

Then he steadied himself and laughed scornfully. "That don't prove nothin'," he said sarcastically. "I've read up on Indians. I know that many squaws paint the parts of their hair red. Where did you get the paint you used on *your* part?"

Frustration turning slowly to rage, Misshi flipped her hair back across her shoulders as she lifted her eyes again to her brother's. "Dale Scott Bradley," she said. "I noticed that you haven't grown out of your lisp. You still lisp when you say certain words, just as you did when you said my true name, Mitzi, when I was born. That is why I am still called Misshi. It became the only name anyone ever called me."

She wiped tears from her eyes as she stepped closer to Dale. She could see his reaction to what she had just said; his own eyes were filled with tears.

Finally, Misshi had reached the part of him that was still the little boy who had loved his baby sister Misshi.

When she saw that the realization of her true identity had him near to collapsing, Misshi almost went to her brother to hold him. But before she could, he had got past his weakness.

Dale had regained his composure all right. But instead of drawing Misshi into his arms, relieved to have finally found his sister, he had visibly recoiled away from her.

"Yes, I'll admit that you are my sister, yet in truth you aren't," Dale said bitterly. "Misshi? Are you still truly called Misshi? Or have you been given an Indian name to suit the dirty, unclean savage that you now are? When I think about the possibility of your lying down with some redskin, with that savage standing beside you, I feel as though I might puke."

Hurt by her brother's reaction, by the way he mocked Soaring Hawk, Misshi at first couldn't find words to respond.

She understood now why the shock of seeing her had almost made him collapse. He'd been shocked

227

because she was dressed as an Indian, had even used some Indian words as she spoke to him. She had lived with Indians and in a sense was now one of them, had even gone so far as to dye her lovely red hair black to make herself look more like them.

Misshi finally found the courage to speak her mind. She took two quick steps toward her brother, standing so close that their breaths mingled as they stared at one another. "Dale Scott Bradley, you disgust me," she said venomously. "I want nothing more to do with you. I have wasted too much energy on you already, pining for you through the years. Not one more minute of my time will be spent thinking of you."

Misshi swallowed hard and fought back the tears that burned in the corners of her eyes. "I . . . I . . . am so glad that our parents did not live to see this side of their son, for they were religious, fairminded people who saw everyone as equal," she gulped out.

Soaring Hawk stepped up next to Misshi and placed a comforting arm around her waist, drawing her back away from her brother.

A smile quivered across Soaring Hawk's lips when he saw that his action had openly repelled her brother even more than seeing her now as an Indian.

Then Soaring Hawk's smile faded and he stood

square-shouldered and proud before the white man. "There has been enough of hurting Misshi's feelings today," he said, his voice drawn. "It will end now."

Chief Washakie stepped up beside Soaring Hawk. "We have come for Chief Bear," he said tightly. "We will take him, or you, Major Bradley, will suffer the consequences. You are holding a mindless old man . . . someone who is incapable of remembering anything of his past. It is inhumane to hold such a man prisoner."

Dale's eyes widened and his mouth parted in a gasp of surprise.

Then he glared at Chief Washakie. "What do you mean by saying that the old renegade is mindless?" he growled out. "What sort of ploy are you trying to use on me *now?*"

"It is true," Soaring Hawk said. He gazed at Misshi. "Do you want to tell him how it happened? Or would you rather I tell him?"

Misshi nodded. "I will tell him," she murmured.

She proceeded to tell her brother about that day so long ago, when she had been abducted before her brother's very eyes, and how a bullet had robbed the old chief of his ability to think, how he could not even remember now the atrocities he had once committed.

229

She explained how Panther Eyes was the one guilty of all the recent massacres.

"Dale, I'm not sure if you know it or not, but it was *your* bullet that entered the base of Chief Bear's skull," she said softly. "I saw you take aim just as I looked back. I saw you take aim, fire, and then I realized that it was your bullet that did the damage to Chief Bear."

She swallowed hard.

"I have never told anyone this before," she went on. "I didn't see the need to tell anyone. But I do now. It was *your* bullet that finally stopped the old chief's vicious ways. Isn't that enough vengeance for you?"

"Then through the years, when I dreamed of the day I would get my revenge on Chief Bear, it was time wasted, because I already had my vengeance?" Dale gulped out.

"Yes, you had already achieved your vengeance," Misshi murmured. "It was the same as if you had killed the man you hated ten years ago."

Misshi could feel both Soaring Hawk's and Washakie's eyes on her. They both knew that if what she had just told her brother was fact, she would have confided in them about it, for it was the sort of truth that was not easy to hold within oneself.

Yes, they knew that it was a lie—a white lie as

she saw it—to help achieve what they all wanted to achieve today.

To take Chief Bear to his wife.

She didn't feel bad about lying to her brother, for to her he was no longer her brother. He was just a man, a fiend, whom she would never claim as blood kin again.

"Well, I'll be damned," Dale said, his eyes dancing. "It was my bullet that took his mind away? I couldn't ask for nothing more than that, now could I? The old goat's brain was scrambled by my bullet?"

He leaned his head back in a fit of laughter, causing a stone-cold silence among Washakie, Soaring Hawk, and Misshi, who now pitied this man more than they loathed him.

Dale's laughter faded. He nodded toward the stockade at the far end of the courtyard. "Follow me," he grunted. "If you want that old buzzard, you can have him. He's worth nothing to me now. Absolutely nothing. Good riddance of bad rubbish, I'd say."

Misshi took Soaring Hawk's hand, and with Washakie walking beside them, they followed Dale.

Dale gave them a look over his shoulder as he continued walking. "But there's no chance in hell you'll get any more of the savages," he growled out.

"You certainly can't have Panther Eyes, especially now that I know he was the true ringleader of this group of renegades. I want Panther Eyes, even though I doubt he'll live to see another day. I'm in my right to hold all of the others, at least until they're transported to a stronger prison. I want to gloat over my success as long as I can."

He hurried on to the stockade and ordered the sentry to unlock the door, then stepped aside as Misshi went with Soaring Hawk and Washakie into the dark building.

When the other prisoners saw Washakie and Soaring Hawk, they stiffened and looked away instead of asking for mercy. They knew they would not get it, for both Soaring Hawk and Washakie were against all that these renegades stood for.

Soaring Hawk paid no heed to those who had cowered away from him even though he hated to see any Indian at the mercy of the white man's so-called justice system.

But those who were incarcerated today had taken their chances by wreaking havoc everywhere. They must pay, especially Panther Eyes, who was the most cowardly of all because he had let another man, Chief Bear, be blamed for his own evil deeds.

Tears welled up in Soaring Hawk's eyes as he was taken to his father's cell. Chief Bear was sitting on the floor on a blanket, his legs and arms folded, his eyes fixed straight ahead of him unseeing as he slowly rocked back and forth, humming.

It was hard for Soaring Hawk to see this man, who had at one time been so strong and muscled, now shriveled up and tiny, his thinning hair gray and hanging down to touch the floor behind him.

His eyes had a blankness to them, and then Soaring Hawk saw the scar and his one eye that drooped, recalling the day his father had arrived home with those particular wounds.

Yes, Soaring Hawk was trying hard to keep his composure as he stepped into the cell and knelt down before his father. Oh, how it hurt to see this beaten, mindless man, thin, weak, and stoic.

His father wasn't even aware when Soaring Hawk could no longer hold back his tears and took Chief Bear into his arms. "Father," he cried. "Oh, Father, it is I. It is Soaring Hawk who has come to take you home to Mother."

Fighting back tears that were caused by Soaring Hawk's hurt, rather than Chief Bear's plight, Misshi stepped into the cell and knelt down beside Soaring Hawk. She placed a gentle hand on his arm as he embraced his father.

Misshi's eyes filled with tears. She wished her reunion with her brother had been filled with the same goodness and love that characterized Soaring Hawk's meeting with his father.

She turned slow eyes up to her brother, who stood outside the cell. She shivered when she saw his cold eyes looking at her with loathing.

She guessed by the way he was looking at her that he was wishing she had died that day of her abduction. Perhaps he was even now planning to make sure that she did die.

She knew she couldn't trust Dale ever again.

Chapter Twenty-two

None shall part us from the other,
One in life and death are we;
All in all to one another—
I to thee and thou to me!
Thou the tree and I the flower—
Thou the idol; I the throng,
Thou the day and I the hour—
Thou the singer; I the song!
                    —Gilbert

Unable to get Misshi off his mind, Dale grumbled to himself as he paced nervously back and forth in his office. For a moment or two he would speak aloud, then only mumble beneath his breath.

He was unaware of someone standing in the doorway watching him, seeing him as the true madman he had become.

When he finally felt a presence, he stopped and swung around to glare at First Lieutenant Jack Collins. The other man's hair color matched Dale's own, and his ruddy complexion reminded Dale of himself when he was a little boy who hated freckles.

"What the hell do you want?" Dale shouted as he clasped his hands tightly behind him in order to keep himself from waving a fist in front of Jack's eyes.

"I've been thinking about your decision to give up the old chief to Washakie and Soaring Hawk," Jack said. He moved into the room, the gold buttons at the front of his blue jacket shining in the lamplight.

He nervously ran a hand across the top of his hair. "I'm not sure that was what you would have done if you'd known what I know about your sister and the Bannock chief, Soaring Hawk," he said.

"I saw it, you don't have to tell me," Dale grumbled. "They didn't hide the fact that they feel strongly about one another." He shuddered visibly. "And don't call her my sister ever again to my face. To me she's nothing now but a savage whore who chose redskins over her own blood-kin brother, and who even speaks like a savage!"

"That isn't the worst of it," Jack said, easing himself into a leather chair beside the fireplace where ashes lay cold and gray in the grate.

"Nothing could be worse than my sister becoming a traitor to her own kind," Dale spat out. He sat in the chair behind his desk. He hung his face in his hands. "I'd never have expected anything like this, or . . . or . . . I'd have stayed in Missouri and pursued my dream of becoming an opera star. Now all of those years are wasted, and for what?"

He lifted his head and pounded a fist on his desk top. "All I get out of it is finding a sister who is in truth no longer any kin to me," he said, his voice growing louder with each word.

Jack eased up from his chair and started backing toward the door. "I shouldn't have come," he said, suddenly afraid of Dale. There was a crazed look in his eyes.

"I'll take my leave now," he said guardedly. "I don't think you'd truly want to hear what I came to say, anyhow."

Dale's eyebrows rose.

He jumped up from his chair and hurried around his desk to Jack. He grabbed him by the arm and stopped him just as he reached the door. "I get the idea you *do* have news that I don't know," he said. "Tell me, Jack."

"I'm not sure," Jack gulped out as he searched Dale's eyes.

"You'd best tell me, or by damn, I'll order you to the stockade where you can join the savages," Dale said in a low growl as he reached a hand up and spread his fingers around Jack's throat. He began slowly squeezing. "I've seen the way you just watch during our raids instead of joining in the killing. I let you get away with it up till now, but you'd better not disregard *this* order. You'd best speak up now, Jack, or I'll get my jollies squeezing the life outta you."

"It's about your sister . . . I mean Misshi," Jack choked out as his eyes widened with fear. "She is more to the Bannock chief than you realize. I . . . I . . . heard gossip about it from a friend of mine who lives in Washakie's village. I met him at a trading post the other day. He . . . he told me about a wedding. Misshi's and Soaring Hawk's wedding. They plan to marry soon."

The words struck Dale's heart as though arrows were piercing it.

He fell back away from Jack. "No, no," he mumbled, the color draining from his face.

"Lord, no," he gasped. "How could she?"

He swallowed back the urge to retch and took

another angry step toward Jack. "Why didn't you tell me this sooner?" he shouted, his eyes bulging angrily. "That would have changed everything. I'd never have let the old chief go. Lord, I wouldn't have allowed Washakie or Soaring Hawk, or even Misshi, to leave this place. I'd have imprisoned them all and made up some excuse doing it. Now? They have gone on their merry way, taking the old chief with them."

"I didn't tell you sooner because I knew you would not want to know the kind of person she's become," Jack said as he caressed his sore, throbbing throat. "I thought it would be best if you still believed that she might be dead. In fact, before she arrived here, I had planned to tell you that I had received word she was dead."

"Well, damn it, she *is* dead, in all ways that count," Dale said, again pacing the floor. "But I must make that a reality now, mustn't I?"

"What do you mean?" Jack gasped out.

"That's none of your damn business," Dale said, turning to glare at Jack. "But what *is* your business is my order to take all prisoners from their cells. Get all of those redskins, including Panther Eyes, and tie them to posts in the courtyard."

"What?" Jack gasped. "Why would you order me to do that? We're supposed to wait for a guard detail to transport them to another fort."

239

"Damn it all to hell," Dale shouted. "I can't stand knowing so much. And I can't stand not making someone pay *now*, not later."

"You don't mean to . . ." Jack said, paling. "You aren't going to—"

"Just do as you are told, soldier," Dale shouted. He hurried to his cache of weapons and grabbed his holstered pistols.

"Yes, sir," Jack mumbled, then turned and hurried from the room.

"He'd best do as he's told, or by God, I'll make an example of him for all soldiers at this fort to see," Dale said, stamping from his office.

He went outside and stood in the shadows of his cabin as several of his soldiers busily dug holes in the ground, then slammed thick posts into the holes and secured them with dirt around the bottoms.

Dale smiled wickedly as other soldiers brought out the renegades, old and young alike, and, one by one, tied them to the posts.

Dale's soldiers came and stood around him, their eyes questioning him. No one said anything as he drew his pistols and held one in each hand, aiming at the Indians.

"Watch now, gents, as I take target practice," Dale said with amusement.

He stopped and glared at one of his soldiers who came and stood directly before him.

"What you are doing is insane," First Lieutenant Abraham Jolson said, his eyes challenging Dale as his commander glared at him. "You know that someone will be arriving soon for these Indians. What will you say happened to them after you've killed them? I've ridden with you, Dale, on all of the raids, and I've killed with you. But I can't accept what you're doing here because of the consequences. I don't want to be court-martialed and shot for killing these prisoners. You just can't kill off prisoners."

"Watch me," Dale said, aimed again, and fired his pistol straight at Abraham's chest.

Dale ignored the gasps of horror all around him. He looked over his shoulder at Jack Collins. "Remove him, or join him," he ordered.

So sick to his stomach he could hardly stand on his rubbery legs, Jack nodded and gently dragged Abraham to the side.

Then all went quiet except for the spattering of gunfire as Dale shot at the Indians until they were all dead and hanging limp on the posts.

Dale playfully blew the smoke from the ends of his pistols, then turned to his men. "Now, men, take all of those carcasses and dump them over the side of a high cliff," he said. "Make sure it's at a

241

place where no passersby can see them. And when we're asked by the authorities where they are, we'll say they escaped."

He turned and went to where Panther Eyes hung, limp and covered with blood. "Gotcha, didn't I?" he whispered, then looked into the distance, his eyes narrowing angrily.

"Misshi, you and the young chief are next, for you see, sister sweet, I can't allow a wedding to take place between you and that savage," he snarled.

He strutted back to his office and watched as all proof of the killings were erased, including the blood that covered the ground, which the men covered with dirt.

"My vengeance is about over," he whispered to himself. "Once Misshi and Chief Soaring Hawk are taken care of, I'll be heading for Saint Louis and the opera stage."

His head gently nodding in time with the song he began singing, he practiced for the moment when he would truly shine.

Chapter Twenty-three

Two souls with but a single thought,
Two hearts that beat as one.
                    —Frederick Halm

Soaring Hawk and Misshi stood hand in hand in
Soaring Hawk's tepee, watching White Snow
Feather with her husband. They had arrived only
moments before at the stronghold. White Snow
Feather had been in Soaring Hawk's lodge, anx-
iously awaiting them.

Soaring Hawk would never forget the reunion,
how his mother had gone to her husband as he lay
on a travois behind Lone Wolf's steed.

243

Both Soaring Hawk and Misshi had seen the joy on White Snow Feather's face.

There had even been a trace of recognition in Chief Bear's eyes as White Snow Feather knelt down beside the travois and bent over him, her hands framing his face as she peered through tears at her husband.

And now, after getting his father comfortable on a soft pallet of furs beside the lodge fire, Soaring Hawk was deeply moved by his mother's attentiveness toward his father.

He could see the adoration his mother felt for his father and understood how his father had survived the years after being wounded severely. His wife had cared for him, loved him, and idolized him. Even though his father could not reason anything out anymore, surely deep within his heart he understood the feelings his wife had for him.

Misshi, too, was touched by White Snow Feather's love for the ailing old man, yet she could not help feeling some resentment over this reunion. She would never be reunited with *her* family.

Although Chief Bear had no hand in her father's death, she could not see the fairness of the outcome of that raid that changed so many people's lives. Especially hers.

But she did know that if Chief Bear had not done those things, she would never have had the chance to meet Soaring Hawk, and she knew that if she had never met him, her heart would have been left without a song, for Soaring Hawk was the only man she could ever love.

Yes, she loved Soaring Hawk so much, she knew that everything that had happened in her life had led to the day she came face to face with him.

She knew this, yet she still felt it was unfair that the old chief should win in the end; he had wreaked havoc, had killed and maimed so easily, and still he had his loved ones around him now.

Misshi felt that she could not stand another minute of watching White Snow Feather fuss over a man who was responsible for so many killings. Stifling a sob behind her hand, she broke away from Soaring Hawk and ran from the tepee.

Blinded by tears, she elbowed her way through a crowd that had gathered outside Soaring Hawk's tepee. When she was finally past the throng of people, she made a turn to her left and ran between two tepees, glad to find refuge in the shadows of towering trees. She ran onward until she found a bluff that overlooked the land below.

Sobbing, she flung herself down onto a thick bed of moss that grew out to the edge of the bluff. "What have I done?" she said aloud. "What must Soaring Hawk think! Oh, he will never . . . never . . . understand!"

Stricken by her violent emotions, Misshi did not hear footsteps coming up behind her.

But she did hear when Soaring Hawk spoke, reaching hands down to her waist and lifting her up to face him.

"I do understand," Soaring Hawk said quietly. "I understand how difficult it must be to face the very man who took so much from you. I had hoped you could get past those feelings when you saw my mother and father reunited and realized just how helpless he is now."

"I tried so hard," Misshi said, her voice catching as she searched his eyes. "Truly I did. But it is so hard, especially after seeing the person my brother has become because of—"

"Shh," Soaring Hawk soothed as he interrupted her. He bent low and brushed a soft kiss across her lips. "Let us say no more about it. You *will* get past this, and then you will enter our marriage with no more burdens on your heart."

He drew her closer.

Their eyes met again and held.

"I will have a lodge erected soon for my father and mother," he said. "Then we will be alone. The only ones who will share our lodge will be our children."

He smiled. "Concentrate on us, Misshi, and on the children we will bring into the world," he said softly. "Will it not be the best of times for us? Is that not what life is all about? To find one's perfect mate and to have children born of love?"

"*Huh*, and just being with you makes me realize how easy it will be for me to get past these feelings that are overwhelming me at this moment," Misshi said softly.

"Do you know what feelings are overwhelming me at this moment?" Soaring Hawk asked, his eyes suddenly twinkling.

"I might," Misshi said, slowly smiling. She flicked tears from her eyes with her fingers. "Do those feelings have to do with wanting me?"

"Always," Soaring Hawk said, his hands now in her hair, brushing it back from her face. "My woman, I am consumed heart and soul by my love for you . . . by my need for you."

"Then love me," Misshi murmured as she reached a hand to his lips and slowly ran her fingers over them.

"It would be a perfect way to make you forget your pain, would it not?" he said, his eyes darkening with passion.

She nodded. "Yes, perfect," she whispered as the passion filled those places inside her heart that moments ago had been burdened by resentment.

"I know a private place," Soaring Hawk said huskily as he gathered her up into his arms and carried her away from the bluff. "Rest your head against my chest as I take you there. Close your eyes. Dream of what we will soon share."

Misshi pressed her cheek gently against his chest and smiled as she recalled the first time they made love, their bodies straining together as they were transported to paradise. She trembled as she re-lived it.

And then her eyes opened wide as she heard the thunderous crash of water from somewhere nearby.

She peered through a break in the trees and saw a wondrously colorful rainbow created by the rush-ing of water over a cliff. It was breathtaking.

She sighed contentedly to realize that those ter-rible feelings that had plagued her a short while ago were already a thing of the past. And she knew she had enough willpower to keep from returning to those feelings. To peacefully coexist with White Snow Feather and Chief Bear, she would make herself brush aside all of her resentment toward Chief Bear.

For Soaring Hawk, and for her own sanity, she would be sure that she never again spoke of the past wrongs to her family. She would force Dale from her mind, too, as though he had never ex-isted. He no longer resembled the boy he had been. He was someone to despise . . . to loathe.

"Do you see the beauty of nature that surrounds us?" Soaring Hawk asked as he laid Misshi down on a thick bed of grass.

"No, not really," Misshi said, trying not to giggle when she saw surprise leap into Soaring Hawk's eyes.

"You do not . . . ?" he began, but she brushed a quick kiss across his lips, silencing him.

"All I see is *you*," Misshi said, then giggled softly when she heard him chuckle at the way she had teased him.

"My Misshi," Soaring Hawk said, then lay down beside her.

His hands twined through her hair. He brought her lips to his. He sought her mouth with wildness and desperation, kissing her long and deep.

And then he leaned away from her, and holding her gaze with his, stripped her gently, then stood and let her remove his clothing.

When they were finally nude and on their knees facing one another, Soaring Hawk placed his hands on Misshi's breasts and softly kneaded them until she let her head fall back, closed her eyes, and moaned.

When he bent low and flicked his tongue over her nipples, she inhaled a quivering breath of ecstasy.

Then he placed his hands on her waist, laid her

249

down on the grass, and spread himself over her.

Misshi clung to him as she felt his manhood probing where she was already wet and ready for him. She opened her legs to him and arched and cried out in ecstasy as he entered her in one deep thrust.

With a sob of joy, Misshi gazed up at Soaring Hawk and saw the fire burning in his eyes as he began his rhythmic thrusts within her. Her hands reached up and rediscovered the contours of his face, the slope of his hard jaw, and then his sculpted lips.

She was keenly aware of his passion, awakening every inch of her body, weaving bright threads of excitement through her heart. As his palms moved soothingly and seductively over her body, lifting her up on waves of desire, he bent low and kissed the hollow of her throat.

And then again his mouth sought hers. His mouth was sensuous, hot, demanding. Their kisses were aflame with a building passion.

He wrapped her in his arms and drew her so hard against his muscled body, she gasped.

Soaring Hawk could feel the urgency building within him. He fought hard to hold the ecstasy back until he knew that she had reached that height of pleasure herself. He wanted them to enter the highest realm of pleasure together.

He lowered his mouth. His lips brushed the smooth skin of her breasts. He swirled his tongue slowly over her nipple.

When he heard her draw in her breath sharply and give a little cry of ecstasy, he sucked on the nipple a moment longer, then kissed his way back up to her lips.

As they clung and kissed and moaned out their pleasure, their bodies rocking, and as he pressed endlessly deeper into her yielding folds, they were the only two people in the universe.

Overwhelmed by rapture, Misshi felt her head begin to reel, and she gave a cry of sweet agony, clinging with desperation to Soaring Hawk as their bodies jolted and quivered and they went over the edge into ecstasy together.

Afterwards, Misshi gazed up at Soaring Hawk, who still knelt over her, his eyes devouring her, his arms enfolding her.

"You were so right to bring me here, to make love with me, for everything is magically right again for me," Misshi murmured as she reached up and twined her fingers through his thick black hair.

"For *us*," he said, nodding. "Now we can proceed with our plans of marriage."

"Yes, yes, please let us not wait any longer," Misshi said as he rolled away from her and reached out a hand to help her to her feet.

He drew her into his arms, their naked bodies pressed together. "You do know the custom of the Shoshone and Bannock that a man and woman's vows are sealed after the man sleeps a full night in the woman's lodge?" he asked huskily.

"*Huh*, I do know this," she murmured.

"Then let us go to your lodge now, my woman," he said.

"Are you going to tell your mother before we go?" Misshi asked.

"*Huh*, I will tell not only my mother, but all of my people, so they will know why their chief's lodge is empty of its chief for a full night and day."

He stepped away from her and handed her dress to her. "Let us hurry now and get the telling behind us. We must gather some food to take with us, and then we will stop and bathe in a creek before we reach your village," he said, hurrying into his clothes. "When we arrive at your lodge, we will be ready for a full night alone. Tomorrow morning we will emerge as man and wife."

"I can't believe it is truly happening," Misshi said, laughing softly at how giddy she suddenly felt.

Fully clothed now, she turned to Soaring Hawk, who was dressed as well. "We only recently met and we are now becoming man and wife. It is like a dream come true."

"No, not a dream at all," Soaring Hawk said,

stopping to take her in his arms again. "It is all very, very real."

He lowered his mouth to hers in a sweet, deep kiss, and then they walked hand in hand toward his stronghold.

It seemed only right that all his people were now together again, to hear how the little boy they knew so long ago was about to take a wife.

Although many had died, finally his people were together again. And they had a chief they could trust.

Soaring Hawk vowed silently to himself that he would never let these people down as his father had done.

Chapter Twenty-four

I could not love thee, dear, so much,
Lov'd I not honor more.
—Richard Lovelace

In a state of euphoria at the idea that tomorrow she would be Soaring Hawk's wife, Misshi rode along smiling ear to ear. Things did seem to be coming together for everyone.

Lost in her anticipation of soon being Soaring Hawk's wife, Misshi was not aware that they had left the safety of the mountain and were now making their way across a flat stretch of land toward Washakie's village.

As the sun began to set, they entered a canyon

where there were many cracks and crevices in the towering rock, crevices wide enough for a man and his horse to hide. Misshi's heart almost stopped and a scream was trapped in her throat when several soldiers on horses rode from one of those hiding places to quickly surround her and Soaring Hawk.

Soaring Hawk grabbed Misshi's reins and drew her horse to a halt close to his. He glared at Misshi's brother as Dale trotted closer to them, then laughed throatily.

"Sister mine, I've decided to put you out of your misery once and for all," Dale growled as he went on past Soaring Hawk's steed and sidled his horse up close to Misshi's. He glared at her. "You aren't worth anything anymore. You are nothing but a savage. It's a shame an arrow didn't kill you on the day you were abducted."

Misshi held her breath. She feared more for Soaring Hawk than for herself at this moment. She knew that if he said anything in her defense, Soaring Hawk might be shot on the spot.

She was so glad when he kept his silence even though she could see the heat of anger in his eyes.

Her eyes were drawn back to Dale when he shouted out a command to his men. Several soldiers dismounted and hurried to stand on each side of Soaring Hawk's horse. One of them yanked him from his saddle and threw him hard onto the ground at the feet of the soldiers gathered around him.

Misshi gasped with horror when she saw soldiers pounding four short stakes into the ground. It did not take much thought to guess their purpose. They were being placed there to bind Soaring Hawk.

She turned to Dale, who still sat in his saddle, amusement evident in his green eyes. "You can't!" she gasped out. "Oh, Dale, please don't."

"Before you take your final breath, I mean to let you watch how savages die at the hand of Major Dale Bradley," he said, chuckling. "You can witness your lover's death, and then, sister of mine, *you* will die."

"You are truly insane," Misshi cried, her breath catching in her throat when a soldier came up to the right side of her horse and grabbed her by the wrist, yanking her down from the saddle. Then he forced her to go and stand where Soaring Hawk was being tied to the stakes, spread-cagled on the ground.

Misshi and Soaring Hawk's eyes met and held. Tears streamed down her cheeks. "My darling, I will get you free," she sobbed out. "Somehow, Soaring Hawk, I will get you free."

"The hell you will," Dale shouted as he came up

next to her and grabbed her by an arm.

"Dale, Dale, how can this be you doing these things?" Misshi cried as he forced her beneath a tree.

"Lieutenant Collins, come and give me a hand," Dale shouted at Jack Collins. "And bring me your rope."

Misshi trembled as Lieutenant Collins came with a rope and stood stiffly beside Dale, his golden-brown eyes revealing to Misshi that of all the soldiers he was the only one who felt misgivings about what was happening here today.

Could she possibly have an ally in him?

"Tie her to the tree," Dale ordered as he stepped back from Misshi and clasped his hands together behind him. "Make the knot secure, Jack. I don't want this savage squaw escaping during the night."

"You don't really mean to do this," Jack said, hesitating as he turned the end of the rope nervously in his hands.

"I gave you an order," Dale said flatly. His eyes narrowed dangerously as he glared at Jack. "Do it, or by God, this will be the straw that breaks the camel's back. I'll see that you hang beside Misshi after I tie her to the tree."

Jack gave Misshi an apologetic look that let her know he was against all that was happening here today.

Confident and egotistical, Dale chuckled as he rocked slowly back and forth from his heels to his toes, watching while Jack tied Misshi's wrists together, then tied the other end of the rope to a low-hanging limb overhead.

"*Now* you just try and get free," Dale taunted. "I don't think so, Misshi. No, I don't think so."

"You'll be sorry for what you're doing," Misshi said, her eyes narrowing angrily. "You will pay dearly for this, Dale. When what you have done is discovered, you won't only be court-martialed, you will be hanged."

"I don't think so," Dale said, then walked away from her and joined the other soldiers. "We'll let them suffer for a while. Then I'll slit the chief's throat." He wheeled around and stared at Misshi. "As for her, well, I'm not sure yet how I'll finish her off."

Misshi scarcely breathed as a campfire was built a little distance from her and Soaring Hawk.

She looked at Soaring Hawk, whose ankles and wrists were spread out and tied tightly to the stakes. She could tell by how he clenched and unclenched his hands that the ropes were cutting into his flesh painfully.

When their eyes met, Misshi's heart ached. She was helpless. There was no way on God's earth that she could get herself free, much less rescue the man she loved.

Soaring Hawk was angry at himself for not having been more cautious. He had been lulled into carelessness by thoughts of their night of love-making, and dreams of the morning when they would be man and wife.

As it was now, he did not see how either of them would live to see another sunrise.

He wanted to apologize to Misshi. But he knew that words weren't necessary. She knew how sorry he was to have let her down in such a way.

Unable to bear the sight of her tied to the tree, Soaring Hawk turned his eyes from her.

He glared at the men who were now sitting around the campfire, eating food from their supplies, and passing around a jug of whiskey.

His eyes widened when a thought came to him. If the men drank enough, they might forget about killing him right away. Perhaps someone would come by and see the wrong being done to Misshi and Soaring Hawk.

He knew that several Shoshone warriors had gone to the trading post early in the morning. Surely they would use this pass to return home with their supplies. There were enough of them to overpower the drunken soldiers.

Then Major Dale Bradley and his men would pay for what they had done today.

Soaring Hawk kept that hope alive in his heart as he watched the pass for signs of the warriors.

He stiffened when two of the soldiers, accompanied by Dale, approached carrying burning sticks whose tips glowed orange and hot. His gut twisted with pain when those hot tips were placed on his chest.

The smell of scorched flesh wafted to Misshi in the breeze.

"Dale! Stop! Oh, please stop!" she cried, tears flooding her eyes. "How can you do such a thing?"

Dale only laughed and moved his stick to another spot on Soaring Hawk's chest. Then with the other soldiers he went back to sit and drink by the fire.

Knowing how Soaring Hawk must be suffering, Misshi sobbed out his name. Her jaw tightened with determination and she began wrestling with the ropes.

Her eyes widened when she discovered that the ropes at her wrists were loose. Jack had not tied them securely. Her heart pounding, she began working at the ropes more earnestly. She wondered if Jack had purposely left the ropes loose.

When the ropes finally fell away, Misshi felt an anxiousness she had never felt before. She was free, but she couldn't yet leave to get help. The men were still drinking, joking, and laughing.

But as darkness fell over the land, the soldiers slumped over one by one in a drunken stupor, no longer aware of anything or anyone. Even her brother had passed out.

Her pulse raced as she stepped away from the dangling rope. She was uncertain what to do next.

She doubted that the men would be asleep for long. Silently she hurried over to Soaring Hawk, who had passed out from the terrible pain of his burns. Desperately, Misshi worked at the ropes that bound him, but the knots were too tight.

Also, Soaring Hawk was surely too weak to travel anywhere. She would have to bring back help to free him.

"Washakie," Misshi whispered, looking in the direction of his village. She knew that it wasn't far, yet would she have time to go and get Washakie and his warriors before her brother awakened and found her gone?

She was afraid of what might happen to Soaring Hawk if that happened. But she had no choice except to go there and seek help.

Her knees weak from fear, Misshi ran stealthily to the tethered horses, grabbed the reins of her mare, and led it away from the sleeping soldiers.

Chapter Twenty-five

With you I should love to live,
With you be ready to die.
—Horace

Washakie held Misshi in his arms as she sobbed out the tale of what had happened to her and Soaring Hawk. "They tortured him," she whimpered. "And he was so brave. He did not flinch, blink an eye, or cry out. He is such a brave man." She swallowed hard. "I love him so much."

She stepped back from Washakie with a wildness in her eyes. "I have taken too much time telling you this," she said, her voice breaking. "Washakie, please hurry and call several warriors.

We must get back to the campsite before the soldiers sober up. I'm afraid of what they might do
when they awake."

She left Washakie's tepee with him and
mounted her horse as she waited for him to round
up his warriors.

The men came hurrying out of their lodges,
armed with various weapons. Some carried rifles,
some carried *pogamoggans*, which were war clubs,
and some wore shields made from the tough skin
of a buffalo bull. Others had magnificently carved
bows slung over their shoulders and quivers of arrows at their backs.

No matter the weapon, they would bring Dale
to his knees to beg for mercy. *If* Washakie and his
men arrived in time.

Misshi felt that they would, for the canyon was
not far away. It hadn't taken Misshi long to reach
Washakie's village. It would take the warriors less
time than she, for they set out at a hard gallop,
following the directions she gave them.

And when they drew near the canyon, Misshi
held up her hand, giving a silent command to the
warriors to stop.

She inched her horse forward so that she was at
the lead. She wheeled her steed around and faced
the warriors. "I believe it would be best if we go the
rest of the way on foot," she said.

She had gotten away from the campsite on her horse without alerting those who slept. But the hoofbeats of many horses would surely awaken them.

She couldn't take any chance that they might have time to kill Soaring Hawk before help arrived.

Following her lead without question, the warriors dismounted. They readied their weapons, then moved stealthily through the dark shadows of the canyon walls, where only streaks of moonlight filtered here and there like shimmering ghosts.

As Misshi crept along, the glow of the soldiers' campfire like a beacon luring them onward, her heart began to thump wildly. Soon she would have Soaring Hawk in her arms again. Soon they would be in her tepee where she could tend his wounds.

She stretched her neck to get a better look at the camp. She gulped back a sob when she spotted Soaring Hawk still lying on the ground where he had been bound some hours ago.

She could see that he was either asleep or still unconscious.

Suddenly Washakie held his rifle above his head as a silent instruction for his warriors to stop. Misshi was glad to see him take over, for her knees had grown weak with fear.

"Now!" Washakie ordered in a loud whisper.

Then everything happened so fast, Misshi's head was in a spin.

The camp was surrounded.

All weapons were aimed at the sleeping men.

Washakie and Misshi hurried to Soaring Hawk.

Misshi awakened him with a soft kiss, then smiled reassuringly at him as Washakie's sharp knife split the ropes that had held Soaring Hawk prisoner.

Soaring Hawk was almost too weak to sit up in Misshi's arms, much less stand.

The ropes had cut off the blood to his fingertips long ago. They were so numb, he couldn't even feel Misshi's hands as she tried to urge him to his feet to get him to safety before Washakie gave the order that would awaken the drunken soldiers.

"Darling, we must get you away from here," Misshi whispered.

Her gaze swept over the wounds on his chest again, then looked up and saw his eyelids drooping as if he felt the need to sleep again.

"Soaring Hawk, please wake up. You must come with me," Misshi whispered anxiously.

Washakie had seen Soaring Hawk's weakness and his inability to get up and walk.

He nodded to two warriors, who hurriedly slung their bows over their shoulders, then went and stood on each side of Soaring Hawk. They placed their arms beneath his armpits and helped him to his feet.

Soaring Hawk was dizzy. He stumbled between the two warriors as Misshi hurried on ahead of them to a place where no bullets could reach her and Soaring Hawk.

She sat down, and as Soaring Hawk was laid beside her, she placed his head on her lap and caressed his brow.

She smiled when she heard Washakie's authoritative voice awaken the soldiers. She heard him warn the white eyes that if they so much as leaned toward their weapons, which were for the most part on the ground beside them where they had fallen asleep, his warriors would kill them.

She winced when she heard Dale call Washakie a filthy savage. His voice was a drunken slur.

"White-eyes, listen well to what I say," Washakie growled out to the soldiers. "Especially you, Major Bradley. You should be more careful about who you capture. One more mistake like this and Washakie will forget he is a friendly Shoshone chief. I will come for you, and you will know the extent of my wrath when I am angered. As it is, I want no trouble from the white leader in Washington. I will not kill you tonight. I will let you go back to your fort. But I will report what you have done to Colonel Braddock. It must be his decision what your fate will be."

Dale started to say something, but Washakie stopped him. "Say nothing you will regret later," he warned Dale. "Keep quiet, white-eyes, for as you see, my warriors are ready to kill you. I am a man of peace, but tonight it would please this old chief to see you dead.

"White man who is blood kin to my Misshi, if you ever cross her path again you will regret it," he said stiffly. "And this time I will not leave it up to the white authorities. You will die the way enemies of all red men *should* die. Slowly, painfully, and without an ounce of pity.

"Take all of the soldiers' weapons," Washakie shouted to his warriors. "Take their steeds. Leave them nothing but their drunken breath to keep them company tonight."

Misshi laughed softly at that last command. She would love to see Dale's expression as his guns were taken from him.

"Misshi?"

Soaring Hawk's voice brought Misshi back to him.

"Misshi, I am sorry I could not protect you from your brother," Soaring Hawk said. "It all happened too fast. I was so involved in thinking about making you my wife, I forgot to be cautious. I have too much experience to let my guard down in that way. With you at my side, I should have been doubly alert."

"You can't blame yourself for any of this," Misshi murmured. "And, oh, Soaring Hawk, I'm so sorry that it was my own blood kin that caused all this evil." She swallowed hard. "I can't imagine how it must have felt being tied to those stakes. And . . . and . . . how they tortured you. I felt so utterly helpless. And my brother did these things. He is a madman."

"You waste emotion when you think of him," Soaring Hawk said. "If you can, Misshi, forget him. Pretend he no longer exists."

"*Huh,* that is the only answer," Misshi said, her voice breaking. She glanced up quickly when Washakie came toward her and Soaring Hawk.

When he reached them, he knelt before them. "It is done," he said flatly. "Your brother knows now the wrong he has done and that he must pay, but at the hands of his *own* people, not ours. I made sure the soldiers are all without weapons." He laughed throatily. "Even their horses and their shoes were taken from them. They will have to walk back to their fort, not ride. They will then know the same weakness and exhaustion that you, Soaring Hawk, now feel."

He reached a gentle hand to Soaring Hawk's

ashen cheek. "Can you ride, or do you wish to have a travois made to transport you to your stronghold?"

"I am strong enough to ride," Soaring Hawk said.

As Washakie's hand fell away from his face, Soaring Hawk leaned slowly away from Misshi.

He smiled at Washakie and placed a hand on his shoulder. "But, Washakie, I will not be going to my stronghold," he said, his eyes filled with life again as he waited for Washakie's reaction to his announcement. "I will be going to yours to spend the night in Misshi's lodge. When we leave it the next morning, we will be man and wife."

Washakie's eyes leaped with joy. "You were on your way to my village to spend the night in Misshi's lodge?"

"I still plan to spend what remains of this night with her. That should be enough to seal our vows as man and wife," Soaring Hawk said. Together, Washakie and Misshi helped him to his feet.

"Then come now and let us get you to my daughter's lodge," Washakie said, chuckling as they walked slowly toward the waiting warriors, who were standing guard over the soldiers.

When Misshi got close enough to see her brother, she gave him a lingering, cold stare, then turned away from him and swore this was the last time she would look into his cold, lifeless green eyes. He was a total stranger to her now.

She walked on until she came to her mare. She mounted as Soaring Hawk was helped onto his horse.

As they rode away, Misshi gazed over her shoulder at Jack Collins. She didn't dare smile at him, for she didn't want to give him away to the other soldiers, especially her brother. He was the man responsible for their downfall tonight; it was he who had helped Misshi in her escape.

But when her eyes met Jack's for a moment, she knew that he understood how grateful she was to him, and that she would never forget his kindness.

Afraid that Dale would catch her and Jack staring at one another, Misshi looked quickly ahead again. Then her gaze went to Soaring Hawk, who sat slumped over in his saddle.

A keen sadness swept through her to see him like this. Normally he sat so proud and tall in his saddle.

Soon. Ah, yes, soon he would be himself again, for she would be the best of nurses as she helped him in his recovery.

That was what a wife was for, wasn't it? To see to her husband's every need.

She was filled with joy at the thought that tomorrow she would be able to shout to the heavens that she was Mrs. Chief Soaring Hawk!

Huh, things did have a way of working out in the end, especially when one's love was strong enough to make it so!

Chapter Twenty-six

Let all thy joys be as the month of May,
And all the days be as a marriage day;
Let sorrow, sickness and a troubled mind
Be a stranger to thee.
                            —Frances Quarles
                            "To a Bride"

The tepee smelled fresh and new. The buffalo
hides had been scraped and bleached white by Misshi not long ago. By custom, she renewed her lodge
each spring.

The air was scented with dried rosebuds which
she kept in wooden bowls scattered about the
lodge. Her clothes were folded in stacks at the back

273

of the lodge near where she slept. Her blankets lay near them. Her cooking utensils and supplies were at the opposite side of the lodge.

"I love this place," Misshi murmured as she sat beside Soaring Hawk, who lay on a snow white pelt beside the warmth of her lodge fire. "I have strange feelings knowing that I will soon say good-bye to it forever, for it has been a happy lodge for me."

"You do not have to leave it if you are so proud of it," Soaring Hawk teased.

He had had his fill of buffalo stew and a pudding that Misshi had made from serviceberries and chokeberries, but he was still weak. And even though Misshi was medicating the wounds on his chest, they still throbbed painfully.

His eyes narrowed angrily as he thought of Misshi's evil brother.

Washakie and his warriors were going at daybreak to report Major Bradley's ambush on Soaring Hawk and Misshi. Surely this time the colonel at Fort Bridger would listen to Washakie. Surely he would stop Major Bradley from doing any more harm in the area.

Though Panther Eyes had been proven responsible for much of the murder and mayhem that had occurred, Soaring Hawk knew that the ambush on whites that he and Misshi had come across had not been carried out by Indians. It had been arranged to look like the Shoshone were responsible. But he believed Dale Bradley was really to blame.

Soaring Hawk hoped that Washakie could convince Colonel Braddock that the major must be sent away, or even arrested and put on trial in the white man's courts.

He smiled at the thought of Dale Bradley and his soldiers walking barefoot back to their fort tonight. Each step would increase their fury at being bested by Indians.

"Soaring Hawk, you have surely been thinking of something pleasant these past moments," Misshi said, bringing Soaring Hawk back to the moment and the woman he loved.

"I regret my weakness tonight," Soaring Hawk said. "A man's first full night with his woman, when their marriage is being celebrated, should not be spent with the man on his back, his woman just sitting at his side. You should be lying here while I blanket you with my body, making love to you."

"This is only one night," Misshi murmured. "We have many, many more nights to make up for this one."

"But this is our special night," Soaring Hawk said. He reached over and took her hand. "My woman, I have not even yet played my flute of love for you."

"We have the rest of our lives for you to play

your flute for me," Misshi murmured. She bent low and brushed a soft kiss across his lips. "Shhh. Just let me continue to medicate your wounds. By morning they should feel much better. "By the time the sun sets again in the heavens, you will be well enough to make up for tonight," she said, her eyes dancing.

"Then you will be my wife and I will be your husband," Soaring Hawk said, bringing her hand to his lips and kissing it.

The tenderness of his kiss, and the love so real and beautiful in his voice, made Misshi tingle all over with sweet bliss.

She could hardly wait to make love as man and wife. Surely the pleasure would be twofold what it had been before. Any inhibitions she might have felt before would have flown away in the wind. When they made love, it would be with such passion . . . such heat!

"Now *you* are the one who is filled with thoughts," Soaring Hawk said as he released her hand and gently touched her cheek. "Do you wish to share your thoughts . . . even your dreams . . . with the man who loves you?"

"I just love you so much," Misshi murmured, her gaze soft and sweet on him. "That's what I was thinking about. I . . . just . . . love you so much." She swallowed hard. "And I am so glad that I was able to go for Washakie and bring him back to you in time. I took such a chance leaving you like that, yet I had no real choice."

A slow smile fluttered across her lips. "And then there was that kind soldier who helped me escape," she said. "I shall never forget that golden-eyed, red-headed man. He purposely left the ropes loose so I could free myself. He is responsible, I truly believe, for our being together tonight. I owe him, Soaring Hawk. *We* owe him. I just wish I knew how we could repay him for what he did."

"If your brother and his soldiers are arrested, you can speak up in this soldier's behalf and see that he does not join the others in a white man's jail," Soaring Hawk said. "I, too, shall speak in his behalf."

"Jack Collins," Misshi said, seeing him in her mind's eye as she spoke the name. "His is a name I will never forget. I do hope that we can find a way to repay him."

"Chances are, Misshi, you will never see him again," Soaring Hawk said, his eyes narrowing. "If your brother knows what is good for him, he will leave the area now with his men and never return. Or else—"

"Let's not talk about it anymore," Misshi said, visibly shuddering at the thought of her brother and what he was capable of doing. "Let's just put

277

that all behind us, at least for the rest of the night. Let me rub more medicine on your wounds, and then I shall lie at your side and we will talk some more, but only of sweet things, not ugly."

Soaring Hawk smiled and nodded.

He raised his arms above his head, closed his eyes, and tried not to wince in pain when Misshi softly rubbed more medicine on his wounds.

He was proud of her knowledge of the Shoshone way of healing. She knew so much, no shaman was required to ensure Soaring Hawk's health. He even doubted that there would be any scarring.

Washakie had taught her everything she knew about herbs and roots. He had taught her how to treat everything from rattlesnake bites to gunshot wounds, and even burns such as the ones inflicted on Soaring Hawk's body.

The salve she was gently spreading on him would not only alleviate the pain, but bring down the inflammation as well.

The root to make this salve was called the "black root." It was chewed up and then applied to the burn. The root had a sour, peppery taste, but Misshi welcomed it if it meant that Soaring Hawk would soon be better.

Once all of the wounds were covered with thick black paste, she reached over and washed her hands in a wooden basin.

Thinking that he was asleep, and not wanting to disturb him, Misshi quietly removed all of the medicine as well as the soiled water from the tepee. Then Misshi secured the skin door.

Tired after all the day's events, Misshi stretched out beside Soaring Hawk on the soft cushion of pelts and quietly snuggled up against him.

It gave her such a relaxed, comfortable feeling to be near him in this way.

"My love," she whispered softly, not wanting to awaken him.

"My woman, I am still awake and I heard you. Hear me well. As your husband I will do my best to give you all that befits your station," Soaring Hawk said, turning on his side to face her, yet making sure her body did not come in contact with his aching chest. He moved his hands to her hair and swept soft strands back from her eyes. "I will even bring clothes for you and toys for our children from St. Louis, if that is something that would please you."

"Soaring Hawk, all I want as your wife is your love, devotion, and children born of our love," Misshi murmured. "I do not need fancy clothes from the white world, nor will our children need such toys. Though I was born into the white world, it means nothing to me now. Your world is the one where I truly belong. It was meant for me to

279

be here, so that I could be with *you*. You were meant for me from the moment we were tiny, new seeds in our mothers' wombs."

"Destinies found, destinies savored," Soaring Hawk said, smiling at her. "But now, my woman, you must sleep. I must sleep. With sleep tomorrow will come much faster, and with it, our marriage."

"I wish I could snuggle closer but I know that I can't," Misshi said softly. "But we *can* hold hands."

He leaned over and gave her a soft, sweet kiss, taking her hands. Their sighs of contentment mingled as their eyes closed and they gave themselves to sleep.

Dale Bradley stumbled through the opened gate at Fort Adams. He was cursing beneath his breath and swearing to himself that all of those red savages would pay. He would raid this area with a vengeance that would make his earlier attacks seem mild. He would make it look to Colonel Braddock as if the savages were responsible.

"I will kill, oh, how I will kill!" he ground out.

Although he ached all over from the long walk, and his feet were torn and bleeding, he would not wait for long before placing war paint on his face and bare chest.

Wearing a breechclout and a long, black wig that would disguise him as a savage, he would first steal horses from the corral at an Indian village. Then he would begin a massacre such as the area had never seen before.

He might even find Soaring Hawk's stronghold in the process! He had succeeded in finding Chief Bear's, hadn't he? Surely Soaring Hawk's stronghold would be as easily found.

"Misshi, ah, Misshi, I will also get even with you one of these days," Dale growled.

Jack Collins was staring at Dale, afraid of what tonight's embarrassment would make him do. Jack was ready to break free of this evil man's grip. Before daybreak he would slip away and hightail it clear out of this area, for once he was gone and Dale discovered it, Dale would not rest until he'd tracked him down and killed him.

He would have to be careful, but he would not stay under this madman's command another night.

Chapter Twenty-seven

My heart is like a singing bird!
—Rossetti

Holding hands with Soaring Hawk, stepping out into the sunshine of morning, Misshi beamed with happiness, for she was now married to the man of her dreams. And they were on their way home to his tepee.

Soaring Hawk stood proud, tall and joyous as he walked with Misshi from her tepee into the wondrous sunshine that seemed put in the heavens today just for them.

As he glanced down at her, he was delighted by her loveliness. Her hair hung long and wavy down her back. Her face was radiantly pink, and she seemed not to be able to quit smiling.

She had gone through her clothes and had chosen her favorite dress. It was made of the finest snow-white doeskin. Her close-fitting bodice was adorned with colorful beads and porcupine quills. The skirt of the dress flowed from the waist, down to elaborately embroidered moccasins on her tiny, graceful feet.

His attention was only drawn from Misshi by the sound of thundering hoofbeats.

They paused just outside the lodge and gazed past the village of tepees and the people who were going about their morning chores. Soaring Hawk recognized Chief Washakie approaching on his magnificent steed, with several of his warriors dutifully following him on their own prized mounts.

He had heard Washakie leave just as the morning sun poured its golden glow down the smoke hole overhead. He knew where he and his warriors were going. To Fort Bridger to report on yesterday's ambush.

Washakie had not known that Soaring Hawk had awakened today feeling almost as good as new and could have accompanied him to the fort. But Soaring Hawk knew that Washakie had chosen not to disturb him for other reasons. It was

Soaring Hawk's special time with Misshi; business must come second.

Washakie knew that Soaring Hawk was eager to take his bride to his stronghold and show her off, and Washakie was right. But Soaring Hawk also wanted to take the time to hear about Washakie's meeting with Colonel Braddock. He wanted to hear that Colonel Braddock had agreed that Major Bradley should be reprimanded for what he had done.

As Washakie grew close and Soaring Hawk saw the frown that made the wrinkles deepen in his copper face, the younger man knew that the meeting had not gone well.

Washakie wheeled his horse to a quick halt before Misshi and Soaring Hawk as his warriors continued to their lodges where their wives had food awaiting them.

As Washakie dismounted, giving his reins to a young lad, Soaring Hawk stepped away from Misshi and greeted him.

"Welcome home, Washakie," Soaring Hawk said.

"It is good to be home," Washakie said, yet his voice was sorrowful.

Misshi realized by his behavior that he had come away from the meeting with Colonel Braddock with ill feelings. She hated to hear the details, for surely it would mean that her brother could get away with murder.

Washakie stepped away from Soaring Hawk and put on a smile. "And how is it between you two this morning?" he asked in a teasing fashion. His dark eyes danced. "How does it feel to be man and wife?"

"Wonderful," Misshi said, smiling broadly. "I cannot tell you how proud I am to be Soaring Hawk's wife. It is something that still seems too beautiful to be real."

"It is real enough," Soaring Hawk said, laughing softly as he reached over and took her hand. "And I am the lucky one. Washakie, again thank you for the honor of having your daughter as my wife. When I return home to my stronghold I will send Lone Wolf with my bride price, which has been delayed due to circumstances that—"

Washakie could not hold back his news any longer. He interrupted Soaring Hawk.

"Colonel Braddock did not listen to what I said about the ambush on you and Misshi," Washakie growled. "No matter what I said, Colonel Braddock seemed lost in another world. He was not touched by what I said about Major Bradley's attack, or by how he treated both of you after he ambushed you."

"Are you saying that he ignored everything with

286

a cold heart?" Soaring Hawk said stiffly.

"He not only ignored it, he is not going to do anything about it," Washakie said heatedly. He clenched his hands into tight fists. "When I pointedly asked him if he was going to go and relieve Major Bradley of his duties and punish him for his crimes, he flatly said 'No.' "

"How could he?" Misshi cried, unable to hold back her anger any longer. "How could he ignore what happened? How could he want a man like my brother in charge at Fort Adams? Does he not know that my brother has been given the freedom now to do as he pleases to anyone?"

"What was his excuse for not doing what should be done about Major Bradley?" Soaring Hawk asked, his jaw tight, his eyes flashing with anger.

"He said that he could not, *would* not send Major Bradley away, nor would he arrest him, because the military is shorthanded in these parts," Washakie said. "He said that in time they will find a replacement who is willing to come to this land where, as he put it, 'savages roam and kill mindlessly.' But until a replacement is sent, Major Bradley must stay in charge. The colonel said he had no choice but to allow Major Bradley to remain at his post at the fort."

"And be damned with those he chooses to kill," Misshi said angrily. "How can the colonel be so blind? So uncaring? I thought he was supposed to be the one we could all count on. Now, when he is needed the most, he fails us all. Both my brother and the colonel need to be replaced."

"It would not matter who takes charge of either fort," Washakie said. "No white soldier cares what happens to the Shoshone or the Bannock people. And after all that I have done for whites? It makes no sense. No sense at all. All of my efforts to keep the peace between my people and the white soldiers have been wasted."

"No kindness offered, or given, is ever wasted," Soaring Hawk said. "And it is wrong to allow this one corrupt colonel to negate the goodness you have done. If not for you, many more of our people would have died. No, Washakie. Never regret the goodness you have done."

"You are right," Washakie said, nodding. He smiled slowly. "Now is the time for smiles and happiness. You two, who are very special to me, have much to do today besides talking of gruesome matters with this weary chief. I would invite you to stay and have a feast in your honor, but I know the eagerness you are feeling to take your wife to your stronghold and show her off." He chuckled low. "I am sure you are eager for her to put a woman's touch on your lodge."

"Yes, I do plan to make some changes, but not

many," Misshi said, smiling. "I want the lodge to still be my husband's, for when he is gone, it will be as though he is still there embracing me."

Soaring Hawk smiled down at her. "I welcome anything you choose to do to my lodge to make it yours, for I, too, will enjoy feeling your presence there when you are gone. There will be times when you will be sitting with the women talking and sewing, or doing whatever the women do when they sit amongst themselves."

Misshi looked quickly at Washakie. "My personal things are ready for transporting," she said.

Ah, when she had made her lovely dresses she'd never dreamed they would be worn while married to a handsome chief. Inside her bags were dresses of skins fancifully arranged, adorned with feathers, beads, shells, and porcupine quills, all of which she prized more than any clothes she had worn in the white world.

She was especially proud of two items she had made—a scarlet beaded blanket and scarlet cloth leggings adorned with hawk bells.

She now planned to use her sewing skills to make special garments for her husband. She would make him a breech flap of scarlet cloth, with matching moccasins. She would make him a scarlet-laced chief's coat.

Yes, although she chose Indian attire over what

she had worn in the white world, she adored the scarlet bolts of cloth she had found and traded for at the local trading post. She had a bolt even now in one of her travel bags.

"Could you send someone into my lodge for my bags and secure them to the back of my horse?" she asked, smiling at Washakie.

"It will be done," Washakie said. He looked over his shoulder and nodded toward the young lad who had taken his horse away. "Bird Boy, come. Go inside Misshi's lodge. Get her things. Secure them to Misshi's mare, which is tethered beside Soaring Hawk's strawberry roan. If there is not enough room for everything on Misshi's steed, place the rest on Soaring Hawk's horse."

The boy's eyes lit up to be carrying out the orders of his chief. He hurried into the lodge and came out dragging the heavy buckskin bags.

After they had mounted the horses, a throng of Washakie's people came and stood with him as they bade Misshi and Soaring Hawk farewell.

Trying not to think further on the matter of Colonel Braddock, Misshi smiled and waved at everyone, then rode out of the village alongside Soaring Hawk.

As they journeyed onward, Misshi was aware that Soaring Hawk kept a hand close to his rifle, looking suspiciously from side to side. She understood. If Dale could ambush them once, he might do it a second time.

"I have no choice but to take matters into my own hands," Soaring Hawk suddenly blurted out. "Misshi, I must take you back to Washakie's village where you will be safe while I try to find a way to prove your brother's guilt. I am determined now to stop him. No one is safe in Wyoming land while your brother is free. I must make sure he never harms you again."

"Oh, please, *no*," Misshi said, her heart pounding at the thought of her husband putting himself in danger again.

She didn't want to be made a widow only one day after they had sealed their hearts forever as one!

"It's too dangerous," she said. "How can you forget what my brother did to us? If I hadn't been able to get to Chief Washakie in time, surely you would be dead by now."

"That is exactly why I must go after him," Soaring Hawk said, reaching over and grabbing her reins. He stopped her horse as well as his own. "If your brother attacked his own sister, he will attack anyone. He is a deranged man. And since Colonel Braddock is blind to what this madman is doing, then it is up to me to stop Major Bradley once and for all."

His jaw tightened. "We should have killed them when we had the chance," he said tightly.

"Then *you* would have been killed by Colonel Braddock's soldiers. Please, Soaring Hawk. Give me back my reins. Let's go on to your stronghold."

"I am as anxious as you to go there and show off my new bride, yet I could not do that with an easy heart," Soaring Hawk said. "My wife, I must stop your brother. I must stop him now."

"But how?" Misshi cried. "If you kill him, then your life, *our* lives, would be over. You know that Colonel Braddock would hunt you down and kill you."

"I am going to go about this as peacefully as I can," Soaring Hawk said. "Proof is what we need, Misshi. Proof. Then Colonel Braddock will have to take action."

"But how will you get proof?" Misshi asked.

"I will go to Fort Adams," he said dryly. "I might be able to find some sort of proof of your brother's guilt if I can get into his personal lodge. Usually men with twisted minds keep trophies of their evil doings. Surely I can find something of that nature among your brother's things."

"*Ka*, it's too dangerous," Misshi said, a sob catching in her throat. "You will be stepping into a trap."

"I am going to do this. I *must*," Soaring Hawk

said determinedly. "Now, Misshi, I am going to give you your horse's reins and you are going to turn back in the direction of Washakie's village. I will escort you close enough so that I can see you safely there. Then I will go alone to Fort Adams. I will watch until I see an opportunity to slip inside."

"Please take someone with you to help you," Misshi pleaded. "Let Washakie assign you some men. Please don't do this alone."

"It is a mission for only one man," Soaring Hawk argued. "That man is *me*."

"No, it's not for just one man," Misshi said, lifting her chin stubbornly. "It is work for a man and a woman . . . a man and *wife*. If you refuse to allow Washakie to assign men to help you, then I will assign myself to go with you. I will not budge from this spot, husband, until you say that I can go with you. I will help you search through my brother's things."

Her eyes wavered. "Perhaps while I am in my brother's cabin I will find something of my mother, or father . . . something I can take and keep."

She reached over and placed a gentle hand on his bare arm. "I can help keep you from being caught," she said softly. She slid her hand down his arm, then suddenly yanked her reins from him. "Four eyes are better than two."

Soaring Hawk was quiet for a moment as he studied his wife's face.

Then his lips quivered into a slow smile. "I got more in the bargain than just a wife when I married you," he said, chuckling. "You are a courageous woman."

"Then I can go with you?" Misshi asked anxiously, her eyes wide. "Can I? Please?"

Soaring Hawk sighed heavily, then nodded. "Come," he said, sinking his moccasined heels into the flanks of his horse and riding off. He smiled as she caught up with him and rode at his side.

"*Huh*, wife, you can go with me," he said. "Let us hurry so we can be home tonight and do what my sore body did not allow me to do last night."

Misshi gave him a smiling, mischievous look, then rode onward with him toward Fort Adams.

"While we are at the fort, I plan to release all of the renegade prisoners that are being held there," Soaring Hawk announced.

"You will?" Misshi gulped out. "Then they will be your prisoners?"

"No, I do not want prisoners in my stronghold," Soaring Hawk said. "I believe those who have been incarcerated by the whites will have paid for their crimes. No doubt they have been so mistreated, they will be grateful for any kindness done them."

"You truly believe they won't raid and kill any longer?"

"I truly believe they only want to be joined again with their loved ones."

"That means you will allow them to join their families at your stronghold?"

"I see no other way," Soaring Hawk said thickly. "My kindness will surely cause a change of heart in them. They will join my warriors and work for the good of our land."

Chapter Twenty-eight

One word frees us of all the
Weight and pain of life;
That word is "love."
—Sophocles

The sun had slid past the midpoint in the sky,
leaning more toward the mountains, where soon
its face would be hidden by the towering peaks.

Having stopped only to eat some of the food the
Shoshone women had slipped into one of Misshi's
bags, the newlyweds had reached a bluff that overlooked Fort Adams.

This lookout point was close enough for Soaring
Hawk to examine the activity at the fort. His eye-

brows lifted when he saw no movement anywhere in the courtyard. At this time of the afternoon, the fort should be full of activity.

"Misshi, except for the one sentry guarding the open gate, it seems that no one else is at the fort," Soaring Hawk said. He leaned forward in his saddle to get a better look. "I see no sign of activity at all."

Misshi edged her mare closer to Soaring Hawk. "Maybe that's because they haven't returned to the fort yet. It was a long way to walk," Misshi said, scarcely breathing as she, too, watched for any signs of life beyond the gate. "Or perhaps they are resting after walking all night."

"I doubt that," Soaring Hawk said. "And I also doubt that Washakie's warnings have ended their plans to terrorize the area."

"But their horses were taken from them," Misshi said. "They couldn't get very far without horses."

"If they had no spare horses at their fort, they would steal horses and then go on their way," Soaring Hawk said tightly. His eyes were glued on the sentry, who casually rested his rifle against the gate, then leaned against the stockade and placed his head on his crossed arms, and soon seemed to fall asleep as he stood there.

Soaring Hawk began to hope that he could, indeed, get past the sentry and into the fort without having to kill anyone.

"*Kee-mah*, come," Soaring Hawk said. "We have wasted enough time wondering why we see no one but the sentry. Let us go and learn firsthand if they are there. If we discover they are asleep in their bunks, we shall return to the bluff and keep an eye on the fort until the soldiers do leave. Then we will return to do as we want."

"Perhaps we should just go home," Misshi said.

"I have not come this far to turn back without answers," Soaring Hawk replied. He reached over and placed a gentle hand on her cheek. "If you wish, remain here while I go. If I see that it is safe for you to come, I shall give you a signal."

"No, I don't want to be separated from you," Misshi said, sighing shakily. "Come on, Soaring Hawk. Let's go and see what we can find. I, too, am anxious to see whether there is something at the fort to prove my brother's guilt."

Nodding, Soaring Hawk gripped his reins and wheeled his horse around as Misshi turned hers away from the bluff.

Together they rode down from the steep slope of land, then ventured toward the fort, staying mostly hidden in the shadows of trees. When they reached the end of the forest, they tied their horses' reins to the low branch of a tree.

His rifle clutched in his right hand, Soaring Hawk nodded to Misshi and they moved stealthily through the knee-high, blowing grass.

When they reached the stockade at the back of the fort, they stopped, inhaled deeply. Soaring Hawk gave Misshi a look of reassurance, leaned over, and brushed a quick kiss across her lips. Then they both inched their way along the fence until Soaring Hawk caught sight of the sleeping soldier.

Soaring Hawk smiled smugly and broke away from Misshi, slamming the butt end of his rifle across the soldier's skull and quickly rendering him unconscious.

Together they rushed through the open gate and ran to the closest bunkhouse. They crept along the log wall until they reached a window. Holding his breath, Soaring Hawk peered through the glass.

He exhaled quickly and smiled when he saw that no one was there. Next he glanced at the cabin in the center of the courtyard, which he knew was Dale's private dwelling and office.

"There was no one inside the bunkhouse?" Misshi asked, wishing her heart would slow down a bit, for it was making her feel weak and cowardly. She was the wife of a proud warrior, and she must prove herself worthy of him.

"No. Now let us go and look through your brother's window," Soaring Hawk said, drawing

Misshi with him as he ran to the back of her brother's cabin.

Again Soaring Hawk peered through the window and smiled. "Except for the one sentry, it seems that the soldiers are gone," he said.

"But what if they still haven't returned since last night?" Misshi asked. "What if they arrive while we are in Dale's cabin?"

"Much time has passed since we left them last night," Soaring Hawk said. "They have had time to return home and leave again. Let us go inside and search before they return."

"Of course you are right," Misshi said. "Let's go and see what we can find. And . . . and . . . perhaps I can take something of mother's and father's to have and to cherish, since I have nothing of them now but memories."

"Memories are sometimes better than physical possessions," Soaring Hawk said, then took her hand and hurried on around to the front of the cabin.

After they were inside, Soaring Hawk began rifling through Dale's large oak desk drawers, while Misshi went back to Dale's living quarters.

Tears came to her eyes when she saw lithographs of her mother and father on her brother's nightstand. And then a sob caught in her throat when she spotted a lithograph of herself and her brother as children. Dale was bending down in front of her to give her a kiss.

"Oh, Dale, how could you have changed so much?" she whispered, taking up the lithograph of herself and her brother and smoothing a trembling finger over the glass of the frame. "You were so sweet, so gentle . . ."

"Misshi, come quick!" Soaring Hawk said, the alarm in his voice causing Misshi to drop the lithograph. The glass frame splintered into tiny pieces as it fell against the oak flooring.

Misshi stared at the broken frame, seeing it as a reflection of how things truly were between her and her brother. At this moment, she felt as though one of those slivers of glass were in her heart.

"Misshi, come and see!" Soaring Hawk said as he knelt on the floor where he had found a loose board that he'd pried open.

Misshi ran into the room and stopped abruptly at the grisly sight illuminated by the afternoon sun casting its light through the window.

"No!" Misshi gulped out as she felt bitterness rise into her throat. "Oh, Soaring Hawk, I believe I am going to be sick."

"I have the same feelings," Soaring Hawk said as he continued to stare at the bloody scalps with their assorted hair colors.

"Here is proof of how he kills his victims," Soaring Hawk said thickly as he lifted an arrow from the hole, careful not to allow his flesh to come in contact with its poisoned tip.

He glanced up at Misshi, who stood with wide, tearful eyes and a hand clasped hard over her mouth. "Poison-tipped arrows, Misshi," Soaring Hawk explained. "Such arrows are even more deadly."

"Lord," Misshi gasped out. "How do you know the tips are poisoned?"

"See the dried material on the very tips of the sharpened stone arrowhead?" Soaring Hawk said, pointing toward it.

Misshi nodded.

"The points of these arrowheads have been dipped into a mixture of pulverized ants and the spleen of an animal that has been allowed to decay in the direct rays of the sun," Soaring Hawk said grimly. "This rotten mixture combined with rattlesnake venom is the deadliest of weapons, even deadlier than a ball shot from a firearm."

Misshi fell to her knees beside Soaring Hawk. "Finding these scalps and these arrows proves that my brother has been killing whites and making it look like the work of Indians."

Misshi studied what was hidden beneath the floor more carefully. She gasped when she found mailbags as well as the belongings of travelers.

"My brother and his men have attacked settlers, coaches and mail carriers, as well as innocent Indians," Misshi said, covering a sob with her hand. "He is the worst of criminals. And . . . I . . . am blood kin to such a demon!"

"Your blood is the only thing you share with Major Bradley," Soaring Hawk said. He carefully replaced the poisoned arrow where he had found it.

Then he lifted the board that he had laid aside and placed it over the hole as though no one had disturbed it.

"Why are you doing that?" Misshi asked, her eyes wide. "Shouldn't we take everything from the hole to the colonel at Fort Bridger? Wouldn't that be the proof he needs to believe us?"

"As loyal as he is to the color of the uniform your brother wears, he would never believe we brought these things from your brother's cabin," Soaring Hawk said. "He would think we gathered these things ourselves just to place blame on Dale. No, Misshi, we must leave things as they are. The proof must be found here."

"What are we going to do now?" Misshi asked as he took her gently by an elbow and helped her to her feet.

"First we will go to Washakie and share what we

found with him," Soaring Hawk said as he walked with Misshi to the door. "Then we will all go for Colonel Braddock and bring him here. We will show him firsthand proof of travesties of the most wicked kind."

Just as they got outside, Soaring Hawk looked toward the stockade, where he knew the renegade prisoners would be incarcerated.

He kneaded his brow, then frowned at Misshi. "I would like to go and see how my father's warriors are, but I do not want to let them in on our plan just yet," he said. "I do not trust their silence. Haste is of the essence. We must hurry from this place and return to Washakie's village before nightfall. Then we can ride to Colonel Braddock's fort. We must return to this fort as soon as possible, even if it is the wee hours of morning. We cannot chance your brother somehow discovering we were in his cabin."

As far as he knew, all was as they had found it.

He took care to make sure the sentry would not soon be found should Dale and his men return before Soaring Hawk. As Misshi watched, he dragged the unconscious soldier to the vegetable cellar in the cook's cabin, where no one would think to look for him. After tying and gagging him, Soaring Hawk hid the sentry behind a tall rack of wine bottles, then hurried back to Misshi.

Anxious to get away, Misshi forgot about the broken frame that lay in splinters on the floor of her brother's bedroom.

She was glad to get back on her horse and ride in the direction of Washakie's village. Surely soon this would all be behind them. Once Colonel Braddock was brought to Fort Adams and saw the proof of Major Dale Bradley's madness, her brother's reign of terror would finally be stopped.

The part of her that would always love the boy he had been ached for him, yet the part that knew him now loathed him and was anxious to see him stopped. If it took death to take the evil from his heart, so be it. He wasn't her true brother any longer. He was a stranger who hated mankind.

Chapter Twenty-nine

For Mercy have a human heart,
Pity, a human face,
And Love, the human form divine,
And Peace, the human dress.
—William Blake
"Songs of Innocence" (1789–1790)

Misshi rode beside Soaring Hawk on their way back to Fort Adams with Washakie and his warriors, and Colonel Braddock and his soldiers, following close behind.

Misshi was proud of how Soaring Hawk had spoken his mind to the colonel. He had convinced Colonel Braddock that Dale was responsible for many of the recent attacks on whites and Indians alike. He'd said that if Dale was not stopped he was going to be the eventual cause of a major Indian/white war.

She had stood proudly beside her husband when he further reminded the colonel about how the Crow, Cheyenne, Arapaho, and Sioux had already joined forces against the white soldiers in their area. Soaring Hawk had told the colonel that no soldier should be allowed to antagonize the tribes in Wyoming land. That had been the point that convinced the commander to side with Washakie and Soaring Hawk.

If the Indian tribes could band together, they would have enough manpower to overtake any fort.

The throng of soldiers and warriors thundered through the tall, dew-dampened grass with Misshi and Soaring Hawk leading them toward Fort Adams.

Misshi glanced up at the moon and shivered. There was an orange cast to it tonight, making it look more savage than beautiful.

"Misshi, are you all right?" Soaring Hawk asked, bringing his horse closer to hers. "You seem troubled. Do you want to tell me why?"

"It's Dale," Misshi said. "I just remembered something I did when we were at Dale's cabin. If he arrives home before we get there, he most certainly will find it."

"Find what?" Soaring Hawk asked, lifting an eyebrow.

"I don't know why I didn't remember it earlier," Misshi said. Her eyes wavered. "Soaring Hawk, I broke a frame while we were there. The glass splintered as it hit the floor. Glass went everywhere. But I forgot about it when you called me into Dale's office to see what you had found beneath the flooring. Then we left so quickly, and all I could think about were those scalps and my brother having put them there."

A warning shot through Soaring Hawk. Dale would know that someone had been in his cabin. He might realize that the intruder had discovered his double life. What he might do then was anybody's guess!

But Soaring Hawk did not show his concern to Misshi. She had burdens enough.

"Do not fear," Soaring Hawk said reassuringly. "Even if he has found the broken glass, our force outnumbers his." He looked in the direction of his stronghold. "I would feel better, though, if my warriors were here to join the fight."

"Soon all of this will be behind us," Misshi said. "I'm sure we have enough men to fight off the soldiers of Fort Adams, even if my brother has had time to prepare for battle."

They had no more time to discuss it, for looming ahead in the moonlight was the shape of the fort.

"I see no new sentry standing guard, nor any lamplight in the cabin windows," Soaring Hawk said.

Washakie rode up next to Soaring Hawk. "We are in time," he said. "Major Bradley has not returned. I suggest we set up a post just inside the forest line and wait in the shadows of the trees for his arrival."

"Just in case, I think it would be wise to send a warrior ahead to investigate at the fort," Soaring Hawk suggested, glancing at Colonel Braddock as he came up to Washakie.

Both Washakie and Colonel Braddock agreed, and soon they were all dismounted at the edge of the forest, waiting for Dale's arrival. The scout who'd been sent ahead to the fort had returned with the news that the white pony soldiers were definitely not there.

Misshi rested on her knees in the tall, blowing grass, her eyes watching for any sudden movement. All around her she heard the sounds of firearms being prepared for battle.

She knew how a long-barreled firearm was loaded. First it must be primed from the horn; then

Savage Moon

a charge of powder was put in. The ball was then dropped in on top of the powder, without any wad in between or on top. In this way, one could load and fire very quickly, four or five times in a minute.

She would never forget how valiantly her brother had protected her, firing his rifle over and over again into the advancing renegades that day.

Her thoughts were brought quickly back to the present when she heard the sound of horses arriving. She leaped to her feet and stood trembling beside Soaring Hawk as he glared toward the noise.

"Mount up!" Colonel Braddock commanded his soldiers as he sprang to his saddle. "Prepare for battle!"

That word "battle" caused a lump to rise in Misshi's throat. It was their plan to suddenly leave the darkness of the trees and surround her brother and his men before they knew what was happening. If everything worked out the way it was planned, no one should die.

Soaring Hawk nodded at Washakie, who then gestured silently to his warriors.

Soon all were on their horses and had their chosen weapons ready as the sound of the approaching horses grew closer and closer.

Then suddenly Dale and his men appeared in the moonlight. Gasps of disbelief greeted them.

Dale and those who followed his lead were dressed in breechclouts and moccasins and wore black wigs with beaded bands holding them in place. Each man had a lone eagle feather tied into his wig.

But their appearance was not the reason for the stares and gasps of horror. Several scalps of different colors were tied to the saddle of each soldier, blood still dripping from them, and blood was spattered across the men's bare chests.

"Oh, Lord, no!" Misshi gasped. Trembling uncontrollably, she closed her eyes. The horrible truth of what her brother had become was too much for her to bear.

"Misshi, get control of yourself," Soaring Hawk said hoarsely to her. "Or stay behind while we do what must be done."

Misshi stifled a sob of grief behind a hand, then turned determined eyes to Soaring Hawk.

"I'm all right," she said, not yet able to stop the trembling of her voice. "Let's get this over with. We should hurry before he gets to the gate and can take refuge behind it."

Soaring Hawk reached a comforting hand to her cheek, then drew it away and yanked his rifle from its gunboot. He rode forward with Misshi at his side as Washakie and his men, and Colonel Braddock and his men, made a wide circle, quickly surrounding Dale and his savage soldiers.

"What the hell?" Dale gasped out, his hand freezing in the act of reaching for his rifle when he saw how many weapons were aimed at him.

Colonel Braddock rode up to Dale and personally disarmed him. "You are a disgrace not only to the United States Cavalry but to all mankind," he growled out. He spat on the ground next to Dale's horse. "Major Dale Bradley, I arrest you and your soldiers for atrocities that make my blood run cold. I shall advise the courts that you should hang from the end of a rope until dead. You deserve nothing less."

Misshi, with Soaring Hawk close by, rode up on Dale's other side. "Dale, why?" she said, a sob catching in her throat as her gaze slowly swept over him.

Dale only laughed at her, then looked straight ahead, ignoring her.

"If Mother and Father were alive, oh, how ashamed they would be," Misshi said, tears sliding down her cheeks. "Dale, from this moment on you are nothing to me. Not even a memory."

She wheeled her horse around and rode back toward the forest, then stopped when another soldier approached. This man was dressed in his full uniform and showed no signs of having been a part of the night's bloody massacre.

"Jack," Misshi said. "Jack Collins."

"I left my post here at Fort Adams and was on my way to catch a paddlewheeler back to Missouri because I could not stand to participate in your brother's madness," Jack murmured, his golden eyes shining in the moonlight. "But then it dawned on me that neither Dale nor any of the soldiers under his lead would tell what happened to the jailed renegades."

Soaring Hawk and Washakie came up beside Jack in time to hear what he had said.

"What about the renegades?" Soaring Hawk asked, intervening.

"They are the reason I left," Jack said thickly. He hung his head for a moment, swallowed hard, then gazed up at Soaring Hawk. "In another moment of madness, Major Bradley decided to take target practice in the courtyard." He stopped, inhaled another nervous breath, then told them how Dale had ordered the prisoners tied to stakes and shot.

"You will find their bodies thrown over a bluff close by," Jack said stiffly. "I only came back to disclose what had happened to the renegades and to get the proof I needed to seal Dale's fate. I knew of the secret hiding place where he kept the trophies of each raid. I was going to wait until he was gone, get all of the scalps and white people's belongings from beneath his floorboard, and take them to Colonel Braddock. I was going to confess everything to him even though I knew that I would be thrown in jail for what everyone would believe was my part in the earlier crimes. But I'd have died a coward if I had not done what I felt was right."

Jack looked at Misshi. "I am innocent of any wrongdoing, for I refused to kill anyone while on those damnable raids," he said. "But I was forced to ride with the others, to watch. I would have fled long ago, but I was, in a sense, a prisoner. It was by chance that I finally managed to escape."

Jack smiled as he looked past Soaring Hawk and found Dale glaring at him. "Yes, Dale, I was going to turn you in," he said, riding over to him and stopping his horse a few feet from his commander's. "Finally it's over. I'm ready to pay my dues, but only for desertion, not needless killings. But I doubt that you are. In your twisted mind you don't even realize the wrong you have done, so you won't ever believe you should be penalized for it."

Jack turned his horse around and gazed at Misshi again. He sighed heavily. "My father was a colonel in the United States Cavalry," he said thickly. "It had been my dream since I was a small boy to follow in his footsteps."

315

He paused, then said, "I'd have left my post at Fort Adams long ago, but being a deserter is looked upon as the worst sort of cowardice. I refused to desert my post until it became too unbearable to remain. I'm glad now that I did."

"I'll break loose from prison, and when I do, I'll track you down, and by damn, you'll pay for double-crossing me," Dale hissed out.

Misshi rode over to Colonel Braddock's side. "Can you go easy on Jack when you hand down the sentencing?" she asked. "He saved Soaring Hawk's life as well as my own. And you see how he had planned to give you all of the information you needed to arrest Dale. Deep down he's a decent man."

"I'll work something out," Colonel Braddock said, nodding. He smiled at Jack. "I know Jack from way back. I knew his father. We went to the same military school. We had the same dreams. Yes, I know Jack is a decent man."

Jack gave Colonel Braddock a salute and smiled. "I appreciate your kind words and your plans to go easy on me," he said. He dropped his hand to his side. He smiled at Misshi again. "And thank you, fair lady, for speaking up in my behalf. I'll never forget you."

Misshi gave him a sweet smile, then turned to her husband. "Please take me home," she murmured. "Let everyone else take care of the rest."

"Yes, take her on home," Washakie said, riding up to Misshi. He reached a hand out and gently touched her cheek. "Daughter, forget all that you have experienced these past days. Focus on being a wife. I think that is where your heart lies, is it not?"

"Ah, yes," Misshi said. "I am very ready to settle into my life as Soaring Hawk's wife."

"Then be off with you," Washakie said, dropping his hand away from Misshi and using it to gesture toward the mountains. "Soaring Hawk, take my daughter home. Help erase all of this ugliness from her mind and heart."

"I shall erase it all," Soaring Hawk said as Washakie edged his horse away from Misshi. "She will have reasons only to smile after tonight, for our lives together will be all warmth and sunshine."

Misshi gave Washakie a smile, then Jack, and then Colonel Braddock. She made certain not to look at her brother again, for the hurt only got deeper each time she saw the scalps that hung on his saddle.

As she and Soaring Hawk rode away, dawn was just appearing along the horizon. It was a new day and with it came a new life. Finally there would be a semblance of peace in the area. When her

317

brother crept into her mind's eye, she would blink his image away, but she would never forget that sweet boy of long ago who couldn't pronounce the name Mitzi.

"Misshi, Misshi, come and catch crawdads with me, Misshi!" her brother would say, carrying one of their mother's fruit jars down to the creek.

"Misshi, Misshi, come and play hide and seek with me," Dale would say on a warm summer's night when the stars sparkled like diamonds in the sky overhead.

"Misshi, Misshi, come and swim in the creek," Dale would say on those hot summer days when there was no breeze.

Misshi squeezed her eyes tightly closed and wished those memories would truly go away, for they cut deep.

"You *will* be able to forget," Soaring Hawk reassured her as he saw Misshi wrestling with her thoughts. "I promise you, Misshi. There will be so much good in your life, you will have no need to recall the happiness of your past life."

"Yes, and I will be forming new memories that I can draw on when I am old and gray," Misshi said, smiling. "Memories of me and you, darling."

"And our children," Soaring Hawk said, returning her smile.

"Ah, yes, our children," Misshi murmured. "But,

Soaring Hawk, we have to make sure nothing goes wrong inside our children's hearts that will cause them to change into something—"

"Something like your brother?" Soaring Hawk asked, frowning. "Never, Misshi. We will not allow that to happen."

Misshi smiled weakly at him. She knew that she and her brother had been raised with so much love and devotion, yet Dale had still turned into a monster.

She knew that sometimes circumstances one had no control over changed a person's character. If she or Soaring Hawk were taken viciously from their children, how would they react?

The eerie cries of nighthawks distracted Misshi from her worried thoughts. She looked up into the sky and smiled as she watched the birds soaring overhead, so free, so beautiful!

Suddenly she felt free of her fears and thoughts of her past. Like Soaring Hawk's mother so long ago, the soaring nighthawks had given her a sign . . . a sign of renewal.

"I feel so happy," Misshi murmured as she gazed at Soaring Hawk. "For a moment I allowed sorrow to get in the way of that happiness. From this moment on, husband, I will only look forward and think beautiful things. I promise."

He gave her a smile that made all wrongs in the world so very, very right.

"We shall be at our stronghold soon," Soaring Hawk said as he led her up the first mountain pass.

Something made Misshi look over her shoulder to see if anyone was following. She sighed with relief when she saw no one. Once up the mountain and safely at the stronghold, she doubted she would want to leave again for a while. She wanted to feel the safety net of the stronghold.

Yet she would soon hunger to see Washakie again, as well as all of her friends at his village; she knew that no fears would keep her away for long.

Chapter Thirty

Her angel's face
As the great eye of heaven shined bright,
And made a sunshine in the shady place.
—Spenser

Mornings were sweet in Misshi and Soaring Hawk's tepee as they awakened in one another's arms. Even now, after several months had passed, their mornings still began with slow, delicious lovemaking.

Winter was past, as were those ugly times when so many had died. Life was beginning again, and beneath Misshi's heart a precious new life stirred.

Everyone reveled in their new beginnings as the

days grew warm, filled with birdsong and the tantalizing smell of freshly sprouted leaves on the trees.

Soaring Hawk touched Misshi's lips wonderingly with his, then slid his mouth away. "Tell me if I hurt you while making love," he whispered against Misshi's cheek as he moved rhythmically, yet gently, within her. He was very aware of their child nestled within her womb.

Succumbing to the euphoria already claiming her, Misshi twined her arms around his neck and shuddered sensually.

"You are so gentle and sweet, how could anything you do ever hurt me?" she whispered.

She sighed languidly, then drew a ragged breath when he slid a hand between them and kneaded the soft fullness of her breast.

Her nipple throbbed, and currents of warmth shot through her as he swept his tongue around the nipple, then sucked it between his lips.

Misshi was keenly aware of new sensations there of late. Her nipples were more tender than before her pregnancy, and they were larger and darker.

Soaring Hawk drew his mouth away and leaned up so that he could look into her eyes. He stilled his body within hers and gently traced the perfect shape of her lips with a finger.

"Whatever changes your body experiences during your pregnancy, you will never be any less beautiful than that first day I saw you," he said huskily. "My woman, my wife, it seems only yesterday that I first saw you and wanted you. And now? Soon there will be three of us, not two."

"Yes, three," Misshi said, smiling at the thought of a new being in their lodge at night. She would listen to its precious breathing and would never stop marveling over God's goodness to her.

"It stirs my heart to think of you holding and feeding our child," Soaring Hawk said softly. "It will be something to fuel my endurance during those moments I am in council away from the two of you."

"Everything you say, everything you do, makes me love you more and more," Misshi murmured. She drew his lips down against hers. "I want to make love with you before we go our separate ways this morning."

"And what are you going to do while I am in council?" Soaring Hawk asked, again softly thrusting within her, each thrust now causing ecstatic waves of pleasure to spread throughout him.

"I . . . will . . . be picking herbs and flowers for our lodge," Misshi said, finding it hard to think logically while her whole body was overcome by the feverish heat that his lovemaking caused.

"We need no herbs or flowers to sweeten our

lodge," Soaring Hawk said, closing his eyes in ecstasy as he felt the familiar heat spreading in his loins. "You . . . are . . . enough, my wife."

His steel arms enfolded her and drew her even closer to his heat.

She felt his hunger in the hard, seeking pressure of his lips as he kissed her. And then he drew his lips from hers and buried his face in the curve of her neck, his breathing erratic, his heartbeat wild.

"Misshi, my Misshi," Soaring Hawk whispered huskily against her pink flesh.

His hands swept down and clasped her buttocks and molded her sweet body against his as he plunged his manhood more deeply within her. At that moment their stormy passion exploded into ecstasy.

Soaring Hawk's body quivered and quaked as his seed splashed into her.

Misshi clung to him, wild with her own pleasure as her body trembled, overwhelmed by delicious tingling heat.

Panting and still clinging, they lay together for a moment longer; then Soaring Hawk rolled away and stretched out on his back. He reached for Misshi's hand and brought it to his chest where his heart still thudded wildly.

"Feel what you do to me," he said huskily as she splayed her fingers, palm side down, over his chest.

She moved to her knees and bent low to kiss him there. Then she slithered over him and lay atop him. Twining her fingers through his dark, thick hair, she gave him a kiss that made him tremble with renewed desire.

Misshi giggled as she rose and went to the wooden basin where she had prepared water for bathing after their lovemaking.

She dipped a cloth into the water, then brought it to Soaring Hawk and gently bathed his manhood. At her touch it sprang quickly back to full arousal again.

"Do not torture me so," Soaring Hawk said, chuckling as he placed gentle fingers on her shoulders and urged her away from him.

"Then you bathe *me*," Misshi said, handing him the wet cloth.

She stretched out on her back and sighed with pleasure as he bent next to her and slowly, almost meditatingly, washed her where she was still sensitive from their lovemaking.

She was so aroused, the mere touch of his fingers as he grazed her flesh made her tremble with bliss. She knew that she could make love this morning over and over again.

But she knew that men were gathering for council. There was no time for further love play.

"I am clean enough," she said, gently shoving

his hand away, then hurrying to her feet.

"I will go and gather the herbs and flowers, and then when you return home our lodge will smell sweet of wild things, and also delicious from the stew that I will prepare for you," Misshi said, her fringed buckskin dress already over her head.

She combed her fingers through her hair where the black dye was fading and the red was beginning to show.

Then she plopped down onto their thick bed of pelts and blankets and yanked on her white, beaded deerskin moccasins.

She planned to renew her family's clothing every spring, the discarded pieces to be cut up for leggings and breech flaps.

She was already secretly sewing Soaring Hawk a pair of fine antelope-skin leggings worked with porcupine quills. She was also sewing Washakie a fine white elk-skin robe. She loved making things for those she loved.

She watched Soaring Hawk dress himself in a breechclout and moccasins, then stood up and wrapped her arms around his neck to bring his lips down to hers.

"Kiss me again so that I will have your taste on my lips while we are apart," she murmured. "I love you so, Soaring Hawk. It is so hard to be away from you for any amount of time, and the councils you have with your warriors are lengthy."

"Those councils keep our stronghold safe and secure," Soaring Hawk said, then swept his arms around her waist and gave her the kiss her pouting lips were begging for.

He stepped away from her, ran his fingers through his thick black hair, turned to give her another soft smile, then was gone.

Hating to relinquish him to life outside of their tepee, Misshi grabbed up a parfleche bag and left the lodge herself.

Waving a hello to one woman and then another, blowing kisses to children playing outside their lodges, Misshi continued walking away from her tepee. Before leaving the stronghold she stopped and gazed at the council house.

"Oh, well," Misshi whispered to herself, shrugging. "I *do* have my own things to do, so I will just do them."

Humming a gentle tune, half skipping through fallen leaves as she entered an area of tall trees, she walked until she came to a place of magical beauty where she could see for miles and miles from a bluff.

The view from the top of this lofty butte inspired her to think about her place in the universe.

The view offered beauty and mystery, and seemed to free her spirit.

In the air came a soft whistling of wind which reminded Misshi of something else. She smiled when she thought of the special night when Soaring Hawk had played the flute of love for her, as he had promised after they first realized their love for one another.

He had made the flute himself out of wood. There were four finger holes above, and one underneath for the thumb. Usually a man played the flute outside a woman's lodge when he wanted to court her. By the various notes, the man could convey plans for meeting her alone in the forest where they would have a tryst.

Misshi hummed the tune now just beneath her breath, smiling as she remembered the huskiness of Soaring Hawk's voice as he had sung it to her just prior to playing the song on his flute.

"I am here waiting for you," he had sung. "I am watched. Remain. I will come again. Meet me tomorrow."

She sighed to herself, stretched her arms over her head, and yawned lazily, enjoying this moment alone amid the wonders of nature.

She never felt truly alone while she was there. God seemed to be with her in every kiss of the soft breeze and sunshine. The smell today was fresh and new from the awakening spring.

Suddenly her heart leaped and she stopped humming. She had heard a sound. She suddenly felt defenseless and anxious.

She realized that she had forgotten to bring the knife which she usually kept strapped to her thigh beneath her skirt. She had forgotten she would need that knife to dig out the roots of some herbs from the ground.

Now she realized her foolishness in leaving the safety of the stronghold without protection.

Yet who could be there? she scoffed to herself. Her husband's warriors were nearby, and no one knew of the location of the stronghold except Washakie.

Her pulse racing, her eyes darting suspiciously from side to side, Misshi took a slow, cautious step forward, then sighed with relief and laughed and felt quite foolish when a deer came out of hiding only a few feet away, then leaped away from her.

"I'm so foolish to be afraid," Misshi whispered to herself, then sighed when she saw a cluster of beautiful purple violets only a few footsteps away. She would take them home and place them in water. Violets had been her mother's favorite flower, and they were Misshi's, too.

Singing one of her mother's lullabies, feeling

carefree and happy, Misshi knelt before the flowers. Just as she reached out to pluck them from their cluster of leaves, a noise behind her made her heart skip a beat and her hand freeze in midair.

"And so here is my savage sister," Dale said, coming around to face her.

In one hand he held a sharp-edged knife. A holster of pistols was belted around his waist.

His face was covered with a thick red beard, and his hair was dirty and greasy as it hung down across his shoulders in thin, twisted wisps.

His clothes were tattered and torn and filthy. And he wore no shoes.

"Dale! Oh Lord, how did you find me?" Misshi asked as she slowly rose to her full height.

She couldn't stop the trembling of her knees, for she knew that Dale could only be there for one purpose. To kill her and Soaring Hawk.

"Dale, how did you find Soaring Hawk's stronghold?"

She gazed quickly down at his bare, bloody, mud-covered feet. "And . . . why . . . are you not wearing any shoes?" she gulped out. "You must have traveled far. Without shoes . . . ?"

She glanced quickly into his squinting green eyes. "Didn't Colonel Braddock arrest you?" she asked, giving him no chance to respond to her other questions. "Did he ignore all of the terrible things you have done?"

"Colonel Braddock is dead," Dale said. "I personally saw to his demise before escaping from his fort. He had recommended that I be hanged for my crimes. Now, I just couldn't let him do that, could I?"

"You . . . killed . . . Colonel Braddock?" Misshi gasped out, knowing that the color had drained from her face. "Are you the only one who escaped?"

"I didn't want to be bothered with anyone else's hide," Dale grumbled. "Only mine." He held out a bare foot. "As for being barefooted? I left with only what you see on my back. When I got the opportunity to knife the colonel, I didn't have shoes on. And I couldn't take the time to take his off. I'd have risked being caught and hanged on the spot for my latest crime."

"But how did you find Soaring Hawk's stronghold?" Misshi said, inching away from him.

If she could just run from Dale and find a place to hide, then Soaring Hawk would miss her and come hunting for her. But that gave her a queasy feeling in the pit of her stomach. Soaring Hawk would be stepping into her brother's trap!

"I had no idea I was anywhere near Soaring Hawk's stronghold," Dale said, moving a step closer to Misshi. "I just knew that I had to get high in the mountains to escape from the military. And, lo and behold, as though by magic, I heard the voice of my sister singing songs to herself, and then found you wandering in the forest, alone. I guess Soaring Hawk's sentries didn't spy me because I came from the opposite side of the mountain from where they are perched."

His gaze swept down and stopped at the slight swell of her stomach. "And it seems I came in time," he said, his eyes darkening as he glared at Misshi. "You're with child. It's going to be a little savage just like you and your savage husband. I can't allow that to happen, now can I?"

"You're going to kill me and my unborn child, aren't you?" Misshi said, feeling more frightened by the minute.

"Good riddance to bad rubbish, as Father would say," Dale said, laughing crazily.

He frowned and thrust the knife into the air close to Misshi's stomach. "Yes, I'm going to kill you and in the process rid the world of one more savage child," Dale hissed out. "Misshi, when I saw you dressed like a squaw, and realized you were in love with the Bannock chief, I knew what I had to do. You are a disgrace, Misshi, to the memory of our father. How could you forget how he died? How you were stolen from me by that renegade chief? How could you have joined the enemy's side by becoming one of them?"

Misshi took another step away from him, then screamed when he made a mad lunge toward her with the knife.

In the next instant, she heard the whizzing sound of an arrow loosed from its bowstring.

She watched, wide-eyed, as the arrow sank into Dale's back, causing him to let out a violent gurgle of pain just before he sank to the ground on his knees. He stared blankly up at her, then fell forward onto his face, dead.

"Soaring Hawk!" Misshi cried as he came running toward her, his bow still in his hand, his quiver of arrows at his back.

"Misshi!" Soaring Hawk cried as she met him halfway and flung herself into his arms.

"How . . . did . . . you know that I was in danger?" Misshi sobbed out, clinging.

"During council, I had a premonition that you weren't safe," Soaring Hawk said, dropping his bow to the ground. He lifted Misshi into his arms and carried her away from her fallen brother. "I had to find you to see if you were in danger." As she clung around his neck, her gaze held his. "My wife, I arrived just in time."

"Yes, in time," Misshi gulped out, closing her eyes and laying her cheek on his bare chest. "He was not only going to kill me, but also our unborn child." She gulped hard. "And then *you*."

"He will kill no one else," Soaring Hawk said as he glared at Dale. "But how did he get here? How did he know about the location of our stronghold? How did he escape the punishment of the white pony soldiers?"

"He killed Colonel Braddock," Misshi said, shivering as she envisioned Colonel Braddock dying at the hands of her crazy brother. "And he never actually found the stronghold. He just happened to have chosen this mountain for his hideout. He would have found the stronghold soon, though."

"He will harm no one else," Soaring Hawk said thickly.

"Are you certain he is dead?" Misshi asked, her voice breaking. "Seems that men like him can't truly die."

"Come with me and see," Soaring Hawk said, putting her on the ground. "It is best that you take one more look. It is best that you see for yourself that he is dead, as are the demons inside him that led him to do the wicked things he has done."

Misshi sought deep inside herself for the courage she needed to go and take a closer look at Dale. She knew that she must see that he was dead, or doubt it forever.

Trembling, her knees weak and rubbery, she

crept closer to Dale, then knelt at his side and shivered. His green eyes were locked in a death stare, seemingly looking at her, yet seeing nothing any longer.

"Yes, he is dead," Misshi said, fighting back a rush of memories. She would not allow herself to think of those good times ever again.

"*Tah-mah*, big brother, who was the *true* savage?" she said, her voice breaking. "You were, Dale. *You* were."

A warm, comforting hand fell upon her shoulder.

She turned tearful eyes up at Soaring Hawk.

"Come now, let us go home," he said thickly.

"But what about him?" Misshi murmured, worrying about the shell of what her brother had once been.

"He will be seen to by the roaming animals," Soaring Hawk said, reaching for Misshi and lifting her into his arms. "He deserves nothing better than that."

Misshi nodded, then clung to him as he bent low, grabbed up his bow and placed it over his left shoulder, then took a few more steps and whisked up her parfleche bag.

"Wait a minute," Misshi murmured as she slid out of his arms. She went to the cluster of violets, plucked several stalks, then smiled up at Soaring

Hawk. "I'm ready to go home now. The flowers will help erase the ugliness I just went through."

Soaring Hawk smiled and nodded, and then again swept her into his arms and walked homeward.

Several nighthawks appeared overhead and began soaring and dipping and squawking.

Misshi smiled up at them, then again rested her cheek against her husband's chest. Finally, she felt that the past was truly behind her.

"Our life is now truly free of that madman," Soaring Hawk mumbled.

"Yes, finally. . . ." Misshi said. "I hate that Colonel Braddock died so needlessly," she added, sighing.

"He should have trusted our word earlier about Major Dale Bradley," Soaring Hawk said. "If he had, perhaps the colonel would be alive today."

"And so would countless others whose lives Dale took before he was finally stopped," Misshi said, shuddering.

"But now he will kill no more," Soaring Hawk said.

"*Huh*, no more," Misshi said, and made herself think of other, sweeter things to get past these painful moments of losing a brother whom she had once adored.

"I shall begin making you a delicious stew for

dinner as soon as we get home," Misshi said. "And how did your council go?"

"Well, very well," Soaring Hawk said, laughing softly. As he stepped into the stronghold courtyard, several children came to grab at them both.

"It is good to be home," Misshi said, smiling down at the children, loving them as much as if they were her own.

"Yes, home," Soaring Hawk said, moving on toward their tepee. "Home. . . ."

Chapter Thirty-one

No sooner met, but they looked,
No sooner looked but they loved;
No sooner loved but they sighed,
No sooner sighed but they asked one another the
    reason,
No sooner they knew the reason but they sought
    the remedy.
                              —Shakespeare
                        "As You Like It," Act V

Several months had passed. It was *wee-mush-tu*, hot
moon . . . autumn. It was the day of the Thanksgiving Dance at Soaring Hawk's stronghold. As
was the custom, a hemlock tree had been planted

in the center of the village for the celebration.

Misshi sat with Soaring Hawk on a raised platform covered with soft, thick pelts. The Bannock people were gathered near the hemlock tree. Pride swelled within Misshi's heart today as she gazed down at her tiny baby daughter. She and Soaring Hawk had named her Pretty Hawk in remembrance of the nighthawks that Soaring Hawk had been named after.

Misshi smiled as Soaring Hawk reached over and gently smoothed a corner of the blanket away from his daughter's beautiful face.

Soaring Hawk glanced up at Misshi and smiled, then again admired the brilliant reddish-gold hair that she no longer dyed.

Misshi smiled when she saw her husband staring at her hair, which she wore today in one long braid down her back. "Are you certain you still wish for me not to dye my hair?" she asked. "It does draw attention. Even now I caught you looking at it again."

"Only because I am so drawn to it," Soaring Hawk said. "No. I do not ask you to change the color of your hair. It is a part of my fascination with you."

"But when you first met me you did not know the natural color of my hair, yet you say you were intrigued by me then," Misshi said teasingly. "So are you saying that no matter how I look you will still be intrigued by your wife? When I am old and gray, possibly even fat, will you still be attracted to your wife?"

"My feelings for you, no matter your age, or weight, or even if that lovely hair of yours turns gray, are everlasting," Soaring Hawk said, then turned away from her when he felt movement at his other side.

His mother had just led Soaring Hawk's father to the platform on which Soaring Hawk and Misshi sat, and gently helped him onto it.

"I am glad you chose to come and join the celebration," Soaring Hawk said, smiling at his mother as she sat down between her husband and son. "I am glad you brought Father. Although he will not understand the purpose of the dancing and singing today, he will enjoy it no less."

"Like the child that he has become, he will." White Snow Feather sighed as she reached over and drew a blanket more snugly around her husband's frail, bent shoulders. "But he will always be my husband and your father, and now your child's grandfather. I cherish the moments I have with him."

Tears filled her eyes as she reached over and took one of Soaring Hawk's hands. "Because of you, my son, it is possible for me and your father to be together," she murmured, squeezing his hand affectionately. "Thank you for forgiving the evil he did before he was shot by that white man's bullet. Thank you for still loving him."

"He is not a hard man to love," Soaring Hawk said quietly as he looked past her at his father.

Chief Bear never stopped smiling. He was still as mindless as he had been ever since he was first injured. But there was a happiness in his smile that brought happiness to those around him.

Soaring Hawk was so glad that he had found his mother in her time of trouble. He had said many prayers of thanks to *Wakonda* for this blessing and all the others that filled his life every day, especially his Misshi and now his Pretty Hawk.

"Soaring Hawk, the celebration is about to begin," Misshi said, drawing his eyes forward. "I only wish Washakie were here. That would complete the happiness of this day."

"As you know, Washakie is busy with his own Thanksgiving Celebration among the Shoshone people, but you know that while he is enjoying this time with his people, his thoughts will also be with us," Soaring Hawk said, speaking more softly now because the dance was about to begin.

He reached up and touched six small pearl-like shells that were braided into a lock of his hair at the left side of his face. "Washakie *is* here, in spirit," he said. "He is here with me by way of this special wedding gift he gave me."

He paused, smiled again, then said, "We will go soon and see Washakie and let him share happy moments with our daughter Pretty Hawk. He misses his granddaughter. It is good that I no longer have to keep my stronghold's location a secret, since the worst of the marauders are no longer in the area. Washakie can come as often as he wishes now, as we can feel free to travel there without constant worry of ambushes."

"Yes, let's go soon," Misshi murmured. "I miss Washakie so much."

"There was a special bond between you and Washakie," Soaring Hawk said. "And that comes from his having been the one to rescue you when you were alone and frightened."

"I shall never forget the bond that was forged between me and Washakie that day when he drew me into his arms and gave me, a stranger, a *white* person, such love and reassurance. I shall always remember those special moments. It is because of Washakie that I am here today, giving thanks with my husband and daughter."

"Let us watch now and feel the blessing that comes with the celebration," Soaring Hawk said, taking one more glance at his daughter's tiny face. He was glad to see his daughter's eyes open and gazing back at him with recognition, for although she was only weeks old, she knew her father well.

His shoulders squared proudly, and, filled with wondrous peace, Soaring Hawk took Misshi's hand and watched the men, women, and children form a circle around the newly planted hemlock tree.

Holding hands, they moved around the tree, their feet pounding and keeping time with a low chant, thanking *Wakonda* for his bounty, and begging a continuance of his mercy.

They were accompanied by a lone drum and a rattle. The drum was made like a tambourine without its bells. The skin forming the head was stretched over the hoop while wet and kept there by sinews being passed through it and the hoop. The *wag-ga-mo*, or rattle, being used today was made of a gourd dried with the seeds inside it.

Misshi was nodding her head in time with the chanting, but in her heart she was giving her own thanks to the one above, whether it be her God who heard her first, or *Wakonda*.

All that she knew was that everything in her life was good now. She had everything a woman's heart could desire, especially the man of her dreams. Their love was so strong, nothing could interfere with it.

And then there was their daughter who had been born of this special love.

Yes, Misshi's life was beautiful and sweet. Those nights of terror when the moon became a *savage* moon were behind her.

She no longer thought of Dale as the villain he had become. She no longer thought of him at all.

There was too much beauty in her life for her to dwell on ugliness.

And then there was the Treaty of 1863, which had been signed at Fort Bridger, sealing the friendly relations between the Shoshone and Bannock nations and the United States.

Travel routes would now be safe. Telegraph and overland stage lines would be permitted to cross Shoshone and Bannock country. A railway might even be constructed there.

The amount of compensation for loss of game to the Indians had been determined, and the United States had agreed to pay annually, for twenty years, the sum of ten thousand dollars to each tribe.

This treaty had been signed by Washakie and Soaring Hawk, as well as nine other Indians and two United States Commissioners.

Huh, for now at least, the relations between the red man and white were good, and that made Misshi doubly proud since she was from both worlds.

She felt eyes on her and turned toward Soaring Hawk. She could tell by his gentle smile that he, too, was thinking of the wonders of their love, and the blessings that had come to them from above.

"*Nei-com-mar-pe-ein*, I love you," Misshi whispered to him, feeling joy well up inside when he whispered the same words back to her.

Author's Note

We that loved him so, followed him, honored
   him,
Lived in his mild and magnificent eye,
Learned his great language,
Caught his clear accents,
Made him our pattern, to live, and to die!
                         —Robert Browning
                          "The Last Leader"

In *Savage Moon* I have included one of history's
most famous Indian chiefs—Chief Washakie. Although most of what I have written is fiction, there
are those truths that I would like to point out
about this wonderful Shoshone chief.

He was known to perform extraordinary acts of friendship for white settlers while exhibiting tremendous prowess as a warrior against his people's tribal enemies.

By the 1840s, Washakie was chief of the Eastern Band of Wyoming Shoshone (sometimes called Washakie's Band). Although quite vain (he loved to be the center of elaborate ceremonies), Washakie was kind and generous to whites passing through the Shoshone territory that was under his control.

Nine thousand settlers once signed a document commending Washakie and his Shoshone Band for their kindness and exemplary treatment toward whites.

Even when livestock belonging to whites destroyed Shoshone root and herding grounds, Washakie made sure that no violent repercussions occurred.

True to Indian custom, Washakie married young and had several wives and fathered a large number of children.

When Chief Washakie passed on to the other side, he was given a full military funeral with the honor of "Captain." He was the only full-blooded Indian in the history of the United States to be given this distinction.

Savage Moon

I feel as though I knew Chief Washakie personally after writing about him.

In my mind and heart I see Soaring Hawk and Misshi as just as real!

—Cassie Edwards

Dear Reader,

I hope you enjoyed reading *Savage Moon.* The next book in my *Savage* Series is *Savage Love,* which is about the proud Cree Tribe. It is scheduled to be released in August 2002. You will find much intrigue, romance, and adventure in *Savage Love.* I hope you will buy it and enjoy reading it as much as I enjoyed writing about the interesting customs and lives of the Cree.

Thank you from the bottom of my heart for your support of my *Savage* Series. I love researching and writing about our country's beloved Native Americans.

Always,
Cassie

(You can read more about Cassie Edwards and her books at www.cassieedwards.com.)